A Stolen Kiss

"Oh, Casey, your present is beautiful," she murmured. "Thank you so much." Then her pleased expression faded. "But I feel terrible . . . I don't have a present for you."

"Certainly you have, Laurie." His tone was soft, suggestive. "You don't even have to wrap it up," he added as she started to protest. "I'll take delivery right now."

Laurie knew an instant's panic as she saw his head come down and his lips covered hers. The kiss began as a gentle quest but as Casey felt her response, his mouth hardened, forcing her to obey his will. She trembled as she felt his hands explore her back before they moved purposefully down to pull her even closer.

Laurel felt as if she were drowning in the sweetness of their embrace, knowing in her heart that this moment was the best Christmas gift of all. . . .

HOLIDAY FOR LOVE

by

Glenna Finley

"Salt water cures love
sooner than anything else."

F. MARRYAT, 1840

A SIGNET BOOK
NEW AMERICAN LIBRARY
TIMES MIRROR

SIGNET AND MENTOR BOOKS ARE ALSO AVAILABLE AT DISCOUNTS IN BULK QUANTITY FOR INDUSTRIAL OR SALES-PROMOTIONAL USE. FOR DETAILS, WRITE TO PREMIUM MARKETING DIVISION, NEW AMERICAN LIBRARY, INC., 1301 AVENUE OF THE AMERICAS, NEW YORK, NEW YORK 10019.

SIGNET TRADEMARK REG. U.S. PAT. OFF. AND FOREIGN COUNTRIES
REGISTERED TRADEMARK—MARCA REGISTRADA
HECHO EN CHICAGO, U.S.A.

SIGNET, SIGNET CLASSICS, MENTOR, PLUME AND MERIDIAN BOOKS
are published by The New American Library, Inc.,
1301 Avenue of the Americas, New York, New York 10019.

First Printing, March, 1976

1 2 3 4 5 6 7 8 9

PRINTED IN THE UNITED STATES OF AMERICA

For
one sunny afternoon in Curaçao
and a rainy day in Rio.

HOLIDAY FOR LOVE

Chapter One

Laurel Cavanaugh's first glimpse of the *Ocean Traveler* was the funnel looming majestically over the end of the Long Beach Municipal Pier.

The big "M," standing for Marden Steamship Lines, on the gray stack was illuminated by searchlights in the early evening dusk and looked exactly like the cover illustration on the cruise folder Laurel had just written for her employers. It was only after she paid off her taxi and stood uncertainly at the end of the gangway with her luggage at her feet that she realized the rest of the cruise folder had lost something in the translation to reality.

For one thing, there wasn't a sleek gleaming hull cinched up firmly to the pier in front of her. The powerful tugs which had shoved the *Traveler* into her berths over the years had left a mottled effect on the ship's bow and stern not unlike chickenpox scars on a human victim. After calling the ship a luxurious cruise liner in her advertising copy, Laurel winced when confronted with the workmanlike veteran of the seas.

Happily, the *Traveler* didn't exhibit any other outward signs of debility; her steel deck was alive with longshoremen moving in conjunction with the Gantry crane operators who were stuffing huge containers, one after another, into the gaping cargo holds. Amidships, forklift drivers looked like a line of carrier ants as they deposited pallets of boxed fruit into open cargo hatches just below the passenger decks. Over their heads, a string of Christmas tree lights tried hard to add a festive note to the businesslike surroundings.

Laurel's mouth tightened with annoyance as she stared up at the blinking lights. Now *there* was something that wasn't her fault! No wonder the Marden passenger department was in trouble—Christmas tree lights in a place like that—and half of them burned out to boot!

She was tempted to get out her notebook and make a note of it but another look at her luggage made her decide against the impulse. If she opened her big bag she'd certainly never get it closed again and the prospect of scattering drip-dry unmentionables over the Long Beach pier was not appealing. She could make notes once she got to her cabin. *If* she ever got to her cabin, she amended.

Angrily she glanced up the steep gangway again. Aside from a grizzled guard who was hunched morosely over a telephone at the upper end of it and two lounging crew members wearing waiter's jackets, there was only one individual who could transfer her luggage aboard.

Laurel took a second look at the man's rumpled hair and drooping moustache as he wrote on a clipboard by the telephone. Only when he straightened could she see the three stripes of a ship's officer on the shoulderboards of his shirt.

By then, she decided there was another complaint to put in her report besides superfluous Christmas light displays. She advanced to the bottom step of the gangway and waggled an imperative finger.

"You . . . up there!"

Her hail caught the man in the middle of raking an impatient hand through his dark hair. He frowned down at Laurel—obviously she was shaped wrong for a container and too small to fit on a forklift. Having reached that conclusion, he shouted back, "Sorry, miss. You're too early. Boarding time for passengers is an hour from now. You'll have to come back later." Then he turned his back on her to speak to the guard standing by the phone.

Laurel's eyes widened in disbelief. She wasn't in the habit of having a man turn his back on her. Any man. As the possessor of deep blue eyes, brown hair styled to a glossy cap, plus a short straight nose and a figure that didn't have anything straight about it, she had learned to fend off members of the male sex in her teens and was now an expert at age twenty-three.

She bit her bottom lip and called out again, *"If* it's not too much trouble . . ." Her sarcasm was somewhat spoiled by the warning clang of the power crane as it changed position, but it brought the ship's officer's scowling face to her view again. "Would you mind sending somebody down to carry these bags aboard before I become rooted to this dock?"

That brought him to the head of the gangway, his frame looking more rugged than ever as he peered accusingly down at the luggage in question. Then, reluctantly, he made his way down the ramp toward her. "Okay—I'll have somebody store your bags," he said when he'd reached her level, "but they should have told you . . . passengers don't board for another hour. I take it you are a passenger?" The question showed a definite lack of enthusiasm.

"After your ecstatic welcome," she replied with equal acerbity, "if I were a passenger, I would now be looking for a phone to cancel my passage. Unfortunately, I work for this company, too. I'm supposed to find the chief purser. His name's Waring—so if you wouldn't mind going to wake him up . . ."

"Look, lady—he's been awake for the last eighteen hours . . . ever since we found these cargo manifests were wrong. There's a little matter of correcting them before we can sail." He was staring down at her with active annoyance. "You must be the woman from the San Francisco office they've foisted on us."

"Well, my name's Cavanaugh . . ."

". . . who's going to tell us what's wrong with the passenger operation." From his tone, he could have been announcing a new shipment of lepers.

She stared back at him with equal dismay and sudden suspicion. "You're on the purser's staff?" she murmured incredulously.

Officers of the Marden Line were supposed to appear in immaculate starched shirts and navy blue uniform coats when in port. She knew because she had written the brochure distributed to the passengers. Also, her illustration of a ship's officer didn't include a thick moustache which looked as if it had been allowed to grow rampantly for weeks rather than face pruning shears.

A man in his early thirties should have more sense, she decided. Her feeling of niggling unease persisted, however, as she asked, "What's your name?"

"Casey," he growled. Laurel's dispassionate survey had brought a flush to his cheeks but his glance didn't waver. Apparently he wasn't particularly thrilled with what he saw either.

She felt a surge of relief. "I see. Well, perhaps you could tell me where to find the chief purser."

He rubbed the back of his neck wearily. "You're looking at him, Miss Cavanaugh. I'm Casey Waring . . . but you can forget the last part. We're an informal bunch aboard the *Traveler*." His glance slid over her in a masculine appraisal that brought her chin up. "What comes before Cavanaugh?"

She bit back an impulse to snap "Miss" and said stiffly, "My first name's Laurel. I'm sorry to be early. I didn't think that employees of the company had to board with the passengers."

"We've never had anyone quite like you," he said picking up her bags and jerking his head for her to precede him up the gangway. "I'm not sure whether you're in the fish or fowl category. Is this a working vacation or do you have a friend on the board of directors?"

She stopped so suddenly on the steep ramp that he almost ran into her. "Let's get one thing straight right now, Mr. Waring. I may be working under you on this trip but I don't have to listen to your innuendos. The board of directors booked me on the *Traveler* because our passenger operation is a disaster area. Since you're chief purser on this ship, passengers are your responsibility . . ."

"I'm well aware of it. Could we continue the catalogue of my responsibilities at another time, Miss Cavanaugh? I don't think the guard gives a damn" he jerked his head toward the man lounging at the top of the gangway—"and I know those two new waiters don't. They're still trying to figure out the bow of the ship from the stern."

Reluctantly she moved on up the incline. "I'm merely trying to explain . . ."

"Well, stow it for now. I have other things to do." He dropped the bags at the end of the gangway and addressed the guard. "See if you can find Hal, will you. Tell him to take these bags to 114." As the older man picked up the phone, Casey turned back to Laurel. "Your steward will bring the luggage along later. Follow me and I'll get your stateroom key." He strode off through the wide metal corridor which ran the width of the ship. Laurel barely had time to glance down another corridor where white-jacketed crewmen lounged in doorways before she heard the chief purser's impatient tones again.

"If you don't mind, Miss Cavanaugh. You can take the grand tour after we sail." He was waiting for her at a stairway alongside the elevator. "It's faster to walk," he said when he saw her hesitate. "We're only going one deck."

"Whatever you say." Laurel didn't mention that she was ready to drop after collecting her bags at the Los Angeles Airport and carrying them miles to the cab stand. Especially since she'd done the same procedure in reverse at San Francisco earlier in the afternoon. Grimly she took a deep breath and climbed the stairs at his heels.

One flight up, he shouldered open the heavy

metal door marked POOL DECK. Laurel dogtrotted behind him down another metal corridor—narrower this time—with numbered stateroom doors along one side.

"These will be filling up a little later," Casey told her with a casual wave toward the closed doors. "The coast passengers are still out on the Disneyland excursion. They come back when the Los Angeles passengers are boarding," he added, pulling up to unlock a door labeled PURSER'S OFFICE. He disappeared inside, leaving Laurel to hover in the empty hallway. While she waited, she wandered down the corridor into a foyer which boasted a ship's store on one side and a combination barber and beauty shop on the other. Beyond, glass doors revealed an attractive tiled swimming pool with lounge chairs stacked around it.

"*If* you're ready, Miss Cavanaugh . . ." the chief purser said behind her.

She turned hastily and saw him waiting, key in hand. "I'm sorry," she said. "This"—she waved feebly—"all this is very attractive."

"Not bad for a disaster area." The glint in his eyes showed that her earlier comment wasn't going to be forgotten. "Now—if you don't mind—I'd like to get you safely tucked away. There are a lot of things for me to do before we sail."

"Of course, Mr. Waring." Scarlet-faced, she reached for the key. "I can find my stateroom, thanks. It's on this deck, I gather."

"That's right." He eyed her warily but didn't relinquish the key as they went back down the corridor. "Yours isn't one of the luxury cabins—

they're all booked. However, you should be comfortable."

As they passed the stairs amidships, they almost cannoned into an attractive man in his late thirties. Laurel just had time to notice his well-fitting beige suit and the contrast between his immaculate white shirt and his tanned skin, before he smiled and said, "I *knew* things had to improve on this cruise." Then, turning to the purser, "Maybe you had plans for yourself, Casey? I'm ashamed of you. That's no way to treat your old friends. Besides," he poked a forefinger toward Waring's chest, "passengers have a priority on these trips. I've been reading your publicity."

Casey made an impatient gesture. "Then you two should have a lot in common. Miss Cavanaugh here writes it. Laurel Cavanaugh . . . Eduardo Grayson. Eduardo's going as far as Lima with us this trip."

Eduardo's eyebrow went up at his terse introduction. "Thanks a lot, my friend. I'll do as much for you some time." He turned back to Laurel and said with the faintest of accents, "Pay no attention to Casey's manners. We have plenty of time on the cruise to fill in all the necessary details."

Laurel took a confused step backward. "I'm not sure about that. This is a working vacation for me, Mr. Grayson."

He waved that aside. "Don't worry about such trivialities. Casey should have told you that I'm one of Marden's better customers."

Laurel looked inquiringly at the purser.

Casey nodded before remarking calmly, "You must be losing your touch, Eduardo. You've never needed to pull rank before."

The jibe didn't bother the other man. "I'm just saving time with Laurel. A two-week cruise isn't a lifetime."

Casey glanced at his watch. "Well, if that cargo doesn't get loaded, we may spend the whole time here at the dock."

"Then why don't you get back to your duties ... I can help Miss Cavanaugh get acquainted with the ship."

"Really, I can fend for myself," Laurel put in. She held out her hand again for her stateroom key. "We can talk another time, Mr. Waring."

"All right. What about after breakfast tomorrow morning . . . around ten in my day room." He looked as if he wanted to say something else to Eduardo who was lingering purposefully, but he changed his mind and headed for the stairs.

"Well ..." Laurel shifted uncomfortably and then smiled at Eduardo. "I'd better find my cabin."

His brown eyes gleamed. "Very well. Shall we meet fifteen minutes from now up in the lounge? It's too bad we don't have time for a drink before dinner but . . ."

"Wait a minute . . . you've lost me."

"Not at all. Dinner will be served fifteen minutes from now and I'll escort you. Casey would take care of the formalities if he weren't so busy. This time, his loss is my gain." He lifted her hand gracefully to his lips. "Fortunately the *Traveler* is small—you'll have no trouble finding me. *Até logo.*"

Eduardo disappeared toward the same stairway and this time, Laurel heard his footsteps echoing on the metal treads as he made his way up to the promenade deck.

She shook her head dazedly. Her first ten minutes aboard the *Traveler* showed that life wasn't going to be dull. Casey Waring obviously couldn't wait to dispense with her company, while Eduardo Grayson's reception couldn't have been more enthusiastic. Of course, she'd heard about South American men and their flattery but this was her first actual experience with it.

She was still smiling as she entered the tiny hallway to her stateroom. Lingering just inside the door, she inspected two shallow closets and then moved on to survey the main stateroom itself. A convertible divan-bunk under the porthole already made up for the night occupied most of the available floor space. Directly opposite, a built-in bureau and mirror provided the rest of the room's amenities except for a small chair at the foot of the bunk. A full-length mirror on another door provided access to a small but well-designed bathroom and stall shower. Laurel checked the abundance of towels and tested the hot water with satisfaction before going back to the stateroom again.

She decided the color scheme of brown and ivory for the curtains, chair, and bureau wouldn't win prizes at a decorators' convention and the brown rug could only be described as "serviceable" at best. On the other hand, she told herself severely as she dropped her purse in the chair and kicked off her shoes, it should do very well. Casey Waring had warned her it wasn't a luxury cabin. And she knew the freight consignment on a cargo-liner ranked higher than the seventy-five passengers who signed on for a round-trip cruise to Peru.

As Laurel hung her topcoat in one of the closets, she took a critical look at the two-piece knit of brown and blue she was wearing. Fortunately, it had lived up to all the manufacturer's claims and was happily unwrinkled. While it wasn't very dressy for her first dinner aboard, the long sleeves and well-fitting lines helped give it a flair. Besides, she told herself as she washed her face and renewed her makeup, ship dinners in port were always informal. Rule One in her passenger brochure confirmed it.

Her bags arrived just as she was leaving the stateroom. A cheerful young man who looked about twenty put them down against the side of the hall corridor and straightened, grinning. "Miss Cavanaugh? I'm Hal, your steward. Sorry you had to wait for these . . ."

"That's all right," she assured him. "I didn't need to change for dinner."

"It's a good thing. Flash was supposed to be on duty—he's another steward—but something must have come up. Mr. Waring sent his apologies."

"I'll bet," Laurel thought derisively. She doubted if the chief purser was in an apologetic mood after trying to rouse a missing steward in addition to his other duties. It didn't fit with the last glimpse she'd had of Waring's stubborn chin.

"Is there anything special you'd like?"

She surfaced as the steward's words penetrated. "I beg your pardon?"

"An early morning call? Fruit in your cabin or a glass of milk at night?"

"Oh, that." She smiled. "Give me a day or two

to find out, will you? I have an idea there'll be so much to eat that I won't need any extras."

"Yes, ma'am. Breakfast's served from eight thirty to nine thirty and dinner's in about ten minutes. You'll hear the gong."

She looked at her watch. "Then I'd better get going. The lounge is up one deck?"

"The main lounge," he confirmed. "Don't worry about locking your stateroom now. I'll take care of it after I've put your bags inside. The only time you have to carry a key is when you're in port."

"I'll remember," she nodded pleasantly. "Thanks, Hal. I'll see you later."

The main lounge of the *Ocean Traveler* gave a hospitable impression with its warm decor. Shades of red predominated on the leather chair coverings and a vivid print of red, black, and white was used to upholster the divans grouped in the corners of the big room. The cheerful print was repeated on the wide curtain panels which covered windows on three sides of the lounge. The drawn curtains, a bright tile mural near the small dance floor in the center of the room, and soft music piped from overhead speakers provided the final touches of informality. Even the rattle of ice cubes in the far corner of the lounge where a bartender worked behind his counter helped shield passengers from the harsh world ashore.

Eduardo, who had been waiting in a chair beside the dance floor, stood up to greet her, "Welcome to our Never-Never Land, Laurel. I was afraid you'd forgotten all about dinner. Either that or you'd decided to jump ship after meeting Casey and me."

She shook her head and smiled back at him.

"Not a chance. Do you know how many people in Marden advertising would like to be in my shoes for this two-week cruise? My only worry was that I might be pushed out of my office window before the time came."

"That makes me feel better," he told her solemnly. Then, waving casually at a group of passengers who were straggling into the lounge from another door, he asked, "Want to start meeting your fellow travelers now or wait until later?"

Laurel quailed at the thought of so many strange faces. "Later, please," she said faintly. "Does it take long to get acquainted?"

"On shipboard!" He burst out laughing. "You must be joking. At sea, all the rules of proper behavior go out the window . . . or should I say porthole."

Laurel was glancing around uneasily. "Why are they all staring at me?"

"Don't worry. After dinner, you'll be old hat," he said, reassuring her. "We'll go outside in the time we have left and see how Casey's cargo is coming along." He led the way to the back of the lounge, shrugging aside one of the glass doors which opened onto a covered afterdeck.

Laurel followed obediently, keeping her eyes averted from the other passengers who were now flocking into the lounge after their day ashore. When Eduardo paused by the rail overlooking the swimming pool and the stern of the ship, she tried to probe gently. "Does it seem to you that most of the passengers are . . . well . . . elderly?"

His broad shoulders started to shake with laughter. "How nicely you put it. I think the average age is ninety-two. Our waiter took one look at them and called it the 'Night of the Living Dead.' And it's the only ship I know where the midnight buffet is served at nine thirty."

She started to laugh. "I can see where my advertising copy will have a new slant from now on."

"Don't make any drastic decisions yet," he warned. "Wait until these people have a day or two at sea—they'll start acting like teen-agers. Too bad we're not going around South America about now. We'd pick up the younger set at Rio. December is the middle of their summer and vacation time. Here in the States most people their age like to stay home during the Christmas holidays."

Laurel started to ask the obvious question and then thought better of it.

Eduardo wasn't deluded by her change of mood. "Go on . . . say it," he urged. "Ask me why I don't stay home at Christmas like the normal person."

"All right. Is there a reason?"

"Certainly. Running away to sea is a pleasant way to escape reality. I've done it every Christmas for seven years now. Ever since my wife died in an automobile accident. It was in Rio on Christmas Eve."

"I'm terribly sorry . . ."

"You learn to live with such things," he said gently. "That was about the time I first met Casey. He started working in the purser's department on freighters during college vacations and afterwards chose to make a career of it. It was a pity when he decided to take a desk job with Marden . . ."

"I didn't know he had. It's strange I haven't seen him ashore."

Eduardo shook his head. "Not really. I understand you're working in their San Francisco branch. Casey's been in the main office in New York until the last few months."

Laurel frowned. "Then what's he doing aboard this ship?"

"You'll have to ask him." Eduardo's kindly features crinkled with knowing laughter. "Wait until he's in a good mood, though."

"Does that ever happen?" Laurel was thinking of her arctic reception from the other man.

"Deus, yes. Casey's one of the most popular officers the company's ever had. You'd be surprised to find how many of these passengers signed up for this cruise just because he's aboard. Besides that, he's Marden's best when it comes to handling cargo. I'm damned glad he's on the *Traveler* this trip—things should get done properly as far as the shippers are concerned."

"I see," Laurel said slowly, wondering if Eduardo knew about the purser's pronounced aversion toward her presence on board. "Mr. Waring certainly looked as if he'd been working hard—I hope he presents a more civilized appearance when he mingles with the passengers. Frankly, I should think he'd have to spruce up a little before the women will be much impressed—" She broke off as Eduardo started laughing. "Now what have I said?"

"It was the thought of Casey needing help with women." He reached out to steady her as the deck suddenly tilted beneath her feet. "Watch out! Hang onto me!" he commanded as Laurel made a surprised clutch at the rail. "I should have warned you. The ship lists when they're putting the containers aboard or discharging cargo." He nodded toward the stern crane which was depositing a container on the afterdeck.

"You mean this teeter-totter happens at every port?"

He looked amused. "Of course. Don't worry, you get used to it. All freighter passengers do." As a chime sounded from the lounge, he added, "There's the gong for dinner . . . shall we go in?"

"All right." She trailed him obediently back through the lounge which was emptying as the other passengers followed the waiter with the dinner chimes straight back to the dining room.

Eduardo saw her smile and grinned in response. "That's another thing about ships . . . food comes at the top of the passengers' priority list. You'll approve of the chefs aboard on this trip. Unfortunately, the new crop of waiters is . . ." he shrugged and went on, "well, you'll see what I mean."

Laurel nodded although she wasn't paying close attention as she paused at the door of the dining salon and peered in. Like the lounge, the decor was directed toward comfortable living. Each table on the deep green carpet was topped with an immaculate white cloth and a bouquet of bronze chrysanthemums. Another bank of floor-to-ceiling windows extended along one side of the room and the maître d' had wisely left the draperies open for the dinner hour so that passengers could observe the colored lights of the busy harbor.

"I had no idea this part would be so luxurious," Laurel said faintly, eyeing the regiment of white-jacketed waiters scurrying around.

Eduardo urged her gently forward. "We'd better sit down or we'll cause a traffic jam."

"But I don't know where to sit. I'd better ask the chief steward . . ."

"That's all taken care of. You're assigned to Dr. Purcell's table with me." He gestured toward a round table for four by the window. "Over there where the blond woman is sitting."

"You'd better lead the way," Laurel said, thoroughly confused by then.

"Nothing I'd like more." He put his hand at her waist and directed her to the table in question. "Miss Cavanaugh, this is Peggy Purcell. Mrs. Purcell is our good doctor's wife." As he reached for Laurel's chair, he turned to the other woman who was an attractive blonde in her early forties, "Laurel does advertising for Marden . . . I told Casey we'd take care of her."

"Oh, I see. Welcome aboard, Miss Cavanaugh." Peggy looked almost as confused as Laurel. "Did you just join the ship?"

"About half an hour ago."

"Well, I'm glad you're with us," Peggy Purcell said before confiding to Eduardo, "I approve of this, but what on earth did you do with Miss Scott?"

He shrugged as he opened his menu. "I told the chief steward to find another spot for her. Miss Scott," he explained to Laurel, "was a singularly boring lady who sat with us last night at dinner when we boarded in San Francisco."

"But . . . I can't take her place!" Laurel exclaimed.

"Of course you can. It's all arranged," he said calmly, looking around the room. "There she is

. . . that untidy brunette next to the empty chair at that big table in the center."

Peggy Purcell's shoulders were shaking with sudden laughter. "The chief purser's table. Eduardo, you fiend! Casey will have her at his elbow for the whole trip. He'll kill you when he finds out!"

"Nonsense—it'll be good for him." Eduardo's attention was back on his menu. "He didn't need Laurel as much as we did."

Laurel tried not to stare at the long table. The brunette, she was relieved to see, appeared delighted with her new assignment. Since Casey Waring's chair was still empty, his reaction was harder to anticipate. Not that he'd be desolate without *her* company, Laurel decided, but Miss Scott and her uncombed hair didn't look like the answer to a man's prayers either. She looked more like a ghastly blind date than anything else.

"It's obvious Eduardo didn't bare his soul when he moved you here," Peggy said, reclaiming Laurel's attention. "Aside from our charming company—we have a small pitfall I should warn you about . . ."

"Our waiter," Eduardo contributed.

"His name's Rip," Peggy went on. "This is his first trip to sea and he only functions at one speed . . ."

"Dead slow," Eduardo finished. He looked up from his menu to advise Laurel, "Make up your mind what you want to eat before he comes. Otherwise he goes into the galley and disappears for hours."

"He's not kidding," Peggy's voice went down to a whisper. "Here he comes now—be careful."

Rip approached carrying a silver ice bucket full of butter. "Evening, Mrs. Purcell. How are you folks tonight?" Then he did a slow double-take as he noted Laurel's features.

Peggy cut in before he could say anything. "Miss Cavanaugh will be sitting with us from now on."

Laurel smiled at the tall, angular boy with his shock of fair hair and thick glasses. "I'm glad to meet you, Rip."

He blinked and smiled—then stared down at the ice bucket as if he were surprised to find it in his hands.

"If we could have some butter, Rip," Peggy Purcell said carefully. "We're all ready to order."

Laurel was amused to note that her patient procedure was followed throughout the entire meal. Rip remained in good humor as he moved doggedly from one course to the next. At times though, the strain apparently was too much and he would disappear into the pantry, eventually emerging with a pitcher of ice water. After Laurel had her glass refilled for the third time, she said to Peg, "I'm beginning to see your problem, but I hate to complain when he's so obliging."

"There's one good thing about it," Eduardo told them. "We'll never be thirsty."

"And we won't have to worry about extra calories. It's just as well. I gained pounds on the last cruise." Peg's gaze turned wistful as she looked over to the purser's table and its inhabitants. "But I'm not surprised Miss Scott is so happy with her transfer. Even with Casey's chair empty tonight."

"Won't Mr. Waring be coming to dinner?" Laurel asked, keeping her tone casual.

"Not when the *Traveler* is due to sail. None of the officers will appear tonight." Peggy looked at her watch. "If Casey's cargo got loaded, we'll leave in another half hour."

Just then they heard the sound of a gong in the hallway outside and a young steward calling, "All visitors ashore, please . . . All visitors ashore."

Eduardo started to laugh and Peggy joined in. She explained to Laurel a moment later, "Last night in San Francisco that steward made a mistake and called 'All passengers ashore.' Miss Scott was ready to abandon ship in the middle of dinner. I thought Eduardo would expire on the spot."

"That's another reason she's happy to have changed tables," Eduardo said, still chuckling. "It'll be a long time before she forgives me. I must confess that after that meal with Rip, I was tempted to transfer to Casey's table myself."

"Our waiter's the reason that my husband is eating dinner in his cabin tonight," Peggy added. "At lunch today, Rip brought in each cup of coffee separately and I thought George would need an analyst or a padded cell before we finally got around to dessert."

"You're sure this is Rip's first trip?" Laurel queried. When Peggy nodded, Laurel went on to explain, "That's too bad. I thought I'd discovered the reason that Marden's passenger business is falling off."

"Oh, that!" Peggy shrugged. "The people at the main office ignore seasonal changes. Our winter cruises going south are always jammed." She nodded toward the end of the room where a table for eight was fully occupied except for a chair in the middle. "Look at that! Captain Samuels always has a harem on his run. Eduardo was supposed to sit there but he reneged," she told Laurel. "We should feel honored. Imagine turning down the captain's table for us."

Eduardo made a rude noise. "He can struggle alone. All those women would be too much for me."

"Hummm. I doubt that." Peggy put her head to one side, considering. "Of course, they're all window-dressing except for the Countess. She's that elegant creature in the black print dress. The Countess de Lazlo . . . originally from Poland and now living in Toronto."

"She seems very attractive," Laurel said after a discreet look toward the captain's table, where she identified a well-dressed woman whose hair was frosted with silver.

"Well, she takes good care of herself. She must be in her early forties, but she could pass for five years younger. Don't you think so, Eduardo?" Peg asked.

"Age doesn't matter that much," he commented as he broke off a piece of roll and buttered it. "She seems pleasant enough, but I've just talked to her once."

"From the look of things, you won't have any chance to know her better. Captain Samuels has put out the word that she's a special friend of his."

"What does the Count de Lazlo have to say about that?" Laurel asked.

"Who knows? Maybe there isn't a Count to ask . . . at any rate he isn't aboard."

Laurel was taking another look at the captain's

table. "That woman with the striking red hair . . . she seems vaguely familiar."

"I shouldn't wonder. That's Gwendolyn Harper . . . she went from starlet roles in the movies to commercials on television. Quite a woman!" Peg added.

"And quite a wardrobe." Laurel was admiring the flamboyant actress's green caftan. "Is she a friend of the captain's too?"

"Not at the moment," Eduardo put in. "I believe she knows some of the other officers," he added tactfully.

"Who all have a wide acquaintance with the female species," Peg admitted. "Even my husband. He was a widower when we were married a year ago," she told Laurel. "This is my third cruise for Marden since then. On the last one, Casey put me to work. You know, addressing invitations for parties, wrapping prizes . . . that sort of thing."

She was interrupted by a young officer wearing the uniform of a second purser, who came hurrying through the room to her side. "Excuse me, Mrs. Purcell . . . I've been told the doctor isn't feeling well. He's resting in his cabin now and they sent me to let you know."

"I see." Peggy's face was pale as she pushed back her chair and rose. "No, don't get up, Eduardo . . . finish your dinner." She turned to the young officer who was still hovering. "Did my husband ask for me?"

"I don't know, ma'am. Mr. Waring thought you should be informed."

"Of course." Some of the tenseness went out of her expression. "Thank you, I'll go right down."

"Is there anything I can do?" Laurel asked when the officer had nodded and left them.

"What's that?" Peggy looked at her blankly as if her thoughts were elsewhere.

"I wondered if there were anything I could do to help. I can address invitations, too . . ." Laurel's voice trailed off as Peggy shook her head.

"Thanks, but it isn't necessary. I'm sure George will be all right in the morning. See you tomorrow."

Laurel stared after her disappearing figure with a puzzled expression which turned to amazement as she felt the increased vibration of the *Traveler's* engines. "Good heavens, I think we're sailing!"

Eduardo glanced at his watch. "On time, too. I told you Casey knew how to handle freight."

"But surely they aren't going to sail when Dr. Purcell is ill. There has to be a qualified doctor on a ship with this many passengers."

"Don't worry about that. Captain Samuels wouldn't be sailing if he thought George was seriously ill. Casey has undoubtedly reported it to the bridge."

Casey again! Laurel decided mutinously. Anyone would think the chief purser was running the ship single-handed. Aloud, she forced herself to say pleasantly, "Mr. Waring sounds so efficient that it's frightening. He'll be walking on water next."

Eduardo merely smiled and took the menu Rip handed him. During the dessert course and coffee, he skillfully kept their conversation on the *Traveler's* itinerary for the next two weeks. Laurel noted thankfully that he made no mention of personalities although he nodded pleasantly to various passengers when they finally finished their dinner and left the room.

"You can meet them tomorrow," he explained to Laurel when an elderly man tried to detain them unsuccessfully. "That fellow's a retired minister from Pasadena and goes into twenty-minute sermons every time he opens his mouth. Tonight I thought you'd have other things to do."

Laurel nodded emphatically. "Lord, yes! I haven't even unpacked. I would like to go out on deck for a minute though. For a last look at land."

"Of course. I forgot that this was new to you. Take the elevator to the top deck and then walk up the last flight of stairs. There's a glassed-in observation bridge with a wonderful view. I'd show you myself but I have to place a ship-to-shore call in the radio room."

"I'm sure I can find it by myself. Will I need a sweater topside?"

"Not if you don't linger too long." He accompanied her out to the foyer and punched the button for the elevator. "I'll see you at breakfast time . . . if not before." Then he reached out to capture her hand and held it lightly. "I think you're going to be one of the nicest Christmas presents I could have asked for. Good night, Laurel."

"Good night. And thank you for making me feel so . . ."—she shook her head helplessly—"is 'welcome' the word I want? It's been a pleasant surprise for me, too."

After he left, Laurel had no trouble following his directions. The elevator took her up to a small passenger lounge decorated in chartreuse and white. Rattan chairs surrounded two bridge tables at the far end while a baby grand piano was bolted to the floor nearby. Long windows on each wall made the lounge especially appealing and tempted Laurel to stay in its cozy atmosphere. Then she shook her head and passed on to a narrow outside stairway.

When she reached the top deck, the view of the receding California coastline made her effort worthwhile. Colored lights made a sparkling display in the Long Beach harbor area and then blended to a predominant band of white on the foothills behind the city. Red warning beacons for aircraft at the top of the hills merely looked festive from such a distance, more like a string of Christmas lights than anything else.

Laurel moved absently around a huge ventilator on the deck which was spewing out warm air from its vents. She was tempted to linger in its balmy drafts and then saw another short flight of stairs. When she had climbed them and made her way around a catwalk above the rail, she came to the glassed-in observation perch that Eduardo had told her about. Delighted with her discovery and the solitude it provided, she slid onto a padded bench to enjoy the scene around her.

Only the faint sound of the *Traveler*'s bow knifing through the calm water and the "Pilot Aboard" flag snapping in the wind at the mast disturbed the marvelous quiet of the night. Overhead, stars matched their man-made counterparts on the California coastline with a dazzling display of their own. The slice of moon gleamed down on the calm ocean bathing its surface spray with an iridescent sheen.

Laurel let out a sigh of utter content.

"Nice, isn't it?" Casey Waring's voice was so quiet that it took Laurel an instant to realize he had come up behind her and was leaning against the end of the padded bench.

"I . . . I didn't hear you," she managed to get out finally. "It *is* all right for me to be up here, isn't it? I mean, it isn't out of bounds for passengers . . ."

"Not at all." She wasn't able to see much of his face in the shadows but there was no mistaking the tone of voice. "It's a free country up here. Not many passengers struggle up all the stairs."

"It's worth it." She started to gesture and then dropped her hand shyly in her lap again. "I like deserted places on ships where you can enjoy the sky and the water."

"I know. I like it myself. As a matter of fact, that's the real joy of being at sea." He rubbed his jaw wearily. "Makes all the other headaches worthwhile. How did you find out about this place?"

"Eduardo . . ." She caught herself, "Mr. Grayson told me."

The chief purser snorted. There was no doubt about it.

Laurel found herself back on the defensive. As if their moment of shared enjoyment had never happened. "Eduardo," she emphasized the name deliberately, "has been very kind."

"I'm sure of that."

"It should be pleasant having him aboard," she added, making sure he got the point.

If he did, he chose to disregard it. "I understand you met Peg Purcell, too. She told me you'd joined their table." He balanced with the ease of long practice as the *Traveler* hit an offshore swell and wallowed in it.

Somewhere on a deck below, Laurel heard the crash of breaking crockery. She clutched at the bench to keep her balance and swallowed nervously.

"Relax, Miss Cavanaugh ... this ship is one of the best riding in the Marden fleet. These swells won't last long," Casey drawled. "How did you happen to end up at the doctor's table?"

"I'm not sure. Eduardo said he'd taken care of it." She broke off as he started to grin. "Did I do something wrong?"

"Nope. Apparently I did. You were supposed to be sitting at my table and now I find myself saddled with Miss Scott. The chief steward sent me a note ... he knew damned well it was safer that way."

Laurel felt a surge of triumph. Apparently she wasn't as unwelcome to him as he'd let on. The next moment, though, her ballooning hopes thudded back to the ground.

"That Scott woman is the biggest bore on the ship. Maybe I can trade her off to the mate. He owes me half a paycheck from the last poker game and there's a blonde from Texas at his table who looks promising." Casey yawned mightily. "Well, I'd better get back to work."

"I hope that Dr. Purcell is feeling better," Laurel said to cover her chagrin. Obviously the chief purser couldn't have cared less about the fact that she wouldn't be sitting beside him. "Eduardo said there was no reason to worry."

"Well, in this case—our Brazilian friend is right. Dr. Purcell will be keeping surgery hours in the morning—I was talking to Peg before I came up here."

"I'm glad." She paused significantly. "It seemed strange to sail under the circumstances . . ."

He frowned down at her. "Don't write all our operations off as a total loss, Miss Cavanaugh. Captain Samuels and the rest of us manage to cope. Or are you looking for omens of disaster?"

"I don't know what you mean."

"If you're serious about finding a reason not to sail . . . we have a covey of women aboard plus a lawyer and a preacher. In the old days, all three categories were taboo."

"But that's absurd . . ."

"Granted. So is the idea of an employee from our advertising department poking her beautiful nose into things she knows nothing about."

She drew back. "There's no need to be so unpleasant, Mr. Waring."

"You're probably right. I apologize." He started to walk away but paused long enough to say over his shoulder, "If you have any more ideas, we have a suggestion box in the galley. Or see Eduardo. He has an excellent technique for dealing with women's problems. And a great deal of experience." The last came out softly.

Laurel ground her teeth together so hard that her jaws hurt. "Don't worry. I'll try not to bother either one of you."

"That's better still. I'll see you at ten in the morning in my day room, Miss Cavanaugh. Sleep well."

"Good night, Mr. Waring." Laurel gazed stonily at the back of his broad shoulders as he went down the short flight of stairs and then disappeared into what was evidently a crew's stair amidships.

She turned back to face the bow, still breathing hard in her anger. Her glance swept blindly over the containers on the deck below and the two huge crates of farm machinery piled in front of them. All she could see was Casey Waring's sardonic expression as he delivered that last rebuke. How could she have thought that the man was beginning to act like a human being!

She climbed stiffly off her bench and slowly walked to the deck below. Before she opened the lounge door, she took a final breath of the tangy salt air. At least the weather was good, she told herself reassuringly. She should be thankful for that.

Too bad that it was the only favorable omen on the voyage so far.

Chapter Two

When Laurel's alarm buzzed the next day, she reached over quickly to turn it off and then lay back for a moment savoring the gentle movement of the bed beneath her. This morning the *Traveler*'s bow was simply quartering the waves and the resultant motion of the ship was easy and undemanding. Nothing to cause anyone trouble, Laurel decided, as she sat up and stretched. When she peered through the big porthole beside her bed, she saw pale morning sunlight sifting through the cloud cover, covering the somber ocean waters and turning the drops of flying spray into jeweled prisms as they splashed against the glass in front of her. Farther forward, the greenish blue surface exploded into white froth when the *Traveler*'s bow sliced through. Then the white turbulence moved outward in a graceful fan shape as the ship passed on.

Laurel could have sat there and stared in fascination for half the morning but the sound of a gong in the corridor brought her startled gaze back to the clock and made her leap out of bed. If she was to have breakfast and be on time for her interview with Casey Waring as well, there wasn't any extra time for daydreaming.

She emerged from her cabin a little later, dressed in trim blue slacks with a white mohair cardigan over her casual blouse. Her steward was lingering in the hall when she paused to lock the door.

"Good morning, Miss Cavanaugh," he greeted her with a friendly grin. "Did you sleep well?"

"Fine, thanks. My only trouble was getting up." She consulted her watch. "There's still time for breakfast, isn't there?"

"Sure thing. But don't worry if you oversleep. The stewardess will bring something down."

"That's good to know. How do I reach her?"

"Call extension sixty on your phone–that's our emergency number. Nobody answers though unless you call between nine and five."

She grinned back at him. "How do they manage to fit all the emergencies into office hours?"

"I've wondered about that myself." He reached down to pick up a pail filled with aerosol cans of glass cleaner and furniture polish. "Maybe you should ask Mr. Waring. Okay if I do your room now?"

"Of course. I'll leave you to it while I find some breakfast. It must be the sea air or something but I'm absolutely starving. See you later."

One deck up, she found the lounge foyer deserted, but a hum of conversation came from the dining room. She made her way through the tables, surprised to be greeted by nods and smiles from the other passengers. There was, she decided as she pulled out her chair, much to be said for the friendliness of cruise passengers. Then she reached for the breakfast menu to be ready when Rip arrived.

When he finally emerged from the galley, she had read it several times, including the fine print on the back which told the history of the Marden Line.

"Morning, Miss Cavanaugh." He was searching laboriously for his pencil as he approached. "Sorry to keep you waiting but I have an extra table this morning and I had to wait for their eggs. Do you want eggs?"

Laurel's visions of a nice soft-boiled egg disappeared at his discouraging tone. If Rip had anything to do with it, the egg would be hard-boiled and stone cold in the bargain. "Just orange juice and a sweet roll with some coffee, I guess," she said regretfully, knowing she couldn't be late for her appointment with the chief purser. "That shouldn't take long, should it?"

"Hard to tell. The pantryman's giving me a bad time this morning. How about grapefruit instead? They're already on the counter."

Her visions of iced orange juice fled along with the egg. "Grapefruit will be fine," she said. "Has Mrs. Purcell eaten yet?"

"No, ma'am. She left word that she'd be having breakfast in her cabin for the rest of the trip. Mr. Grayson said the same thing and the Doc eats his breakfast in the officers' mess. That only leaves you."

"I see."

He started for the galley. "I'll try and get your melon. It may take a while."

Laurel opened her lips to correct him and then sank back in her chair. It was too early in the day to start arguing about grapefruit or melon. If he managed to just get a cup of coffee to her, she'd be content.

When she finally left the dining room and passed through the foyer to knock on the door of the chief purser's day room, the clock in the hallway showed ten minutes past ten.

The metal door in front of her opened promptly.

"You're late, Miss Cavanaugh," were his first words.

"If you'd let me hire some waiters, I'd have been on time," she retorted, brushing past him into the tiny room. "It took me forty-seven minutes before I finally got a cup of . . ." her voice trailed off as she stared at his lounging figure.

Gone was the rumpled, moustached individual who'd snarled at her from the gangway. He'd been replaced by a clean-shaven man in an immaculate white officer's uniform. A man whose hair no longer straggled over his collar but instead had submitted to the recent ministrations of a good barber.

"Good lord, I hardly recognized you," she said in a tone of wonder, still fascinated by his smooth upper lip and the disappearing moustache. "Did you shave it off because it got in the way?" Then she turned scarlet as his eyebrows went up. "I didn't mean . . ." she began.

"The hell you didn't." He shook his head. "Sorry, I shouldn't have said that."

She blinked at his apology. "No—that's my line. I shouldn't have gotten personal."

Casey's grin gave a piratical glint to his features. "No need to prostrate yourself. But to answer the question about the moustache, I didn't have any complaints on that score. Actually I just grew it as the result of a bet. On the last cruise we were away two months, going around South America. Things were a little dull at times and we had to keep the passengers amused." He waved her to a chair under the porthole and sat across from her. "Frankly, it was an awful nuisance."

She kept her tone solemn. "Are you talking about the moustache or the passengers?"

His eyes sparked with laughter. "The passengers were no trouble at all. I only hope we do as well this voyage. That's why I need your help. We had to sail without our social director last night. That may not sound like much of a calamity to you, Miss Cavanaugh . . ." A pained look passed over his face as he broke off to say, "Miss Cavanaugh's an awful mouthful. What do your friends call you?"

"Laurel," she said, stiffening with surprise. "Sometimes Laurie."

"I'll start with Laurel. My name's Casey." With that settled, he went back to his original train of thought. "I'm going to need some help with the social end and the activity schedule. How are you with craft stuff?"

She sighed. "It took me three weeks to make a bean bag in my eighth-grade sewing class and when I knitted an afghan for the Veterans' Hospital last year, they sent it back with a polite note saying it didn't meet their standards."

"That bad, eh?"

She nodded without speaking.

"Can you type?" he asked after a minute.

Her features brightened. "Now you're getting in my league. I've been doing that for years."

"Good. I'll ask Peg to handle the craft classes. You can take over the Good Morning sheet and the office duties. That will just mean a couple hours work in here each forenoon. You can fill in on the shore excursions, too."

"But I've never been to these ports . . ."

"That's all right. We have regular guides for the commentary on the tours. All you have to do is count noses when our people get on the bus." He straightened to look at his watch again. "I think that's everything. You can use the typewriter there," he gestured toward a desk at the end of the room. "The stencils are in the top drawer on the right. I've left a couple copies of past Good Morning sheets out for a guide and some notes for the schedule."

"But I don't even know what the Good Morning sheet is . . ."

"It's the bulletin we distribute to each stateroom listing the day's activities."

"What about the one for today?"

"We'll have to skip it. Never mind, I'll make an announcement in the main lounge when people gather before lunch. All that's on tonight is the captain's cocktail party and a movie after dinner. Nobody will miss the cocktail party because there's free liquor and we send an individual invitation." He paused with his hand on the door knob. "Peg did those yesterday and the stewards will distribute them. Say . . . speaking of stewards, ask around and find out why we're running short of linen on the first day out." He pulled open the door. "Any questions?"

"Just a small one. Are you related to Genghis Khan or is it Alexander the Great?"

He simply grinned. "Would you believe Attila the Hun? If I'm not back when you're finished, just leave the stuff on the desk. And if anybody wants me, I'll be at the office one deck down . . . where I collected your stateroom key last night."

"I remember."

"Good. Then I'll see you later."

Laurel stared after him in bemused fashion for a moment or two and then got slowly to her feet. Somebody should have warned her about the chief purser before she came on board. Her dreams of a carefree vacation time had vanished even as he spoke. At least, her boss in the advertising department would be impressed.

She walked over to the desk and then decided to make a brief investigation of Casey Waring's quarters before she began work.

The small room where she stood obviously served for his official social functions with a compact bar in one corner and upholstered chairs and settee at the far end. A bathroom opened off the short hall which led on to an inner room. There in his personal quarters, a double row of starched uniforms hung from an open closet rack and a single bunk was already made up under the porthole opposite. A high bureau was topped with a pair of military brushes but the only other signs of personal occupancy were a travel clock and some books on a night table.

Feeling as if she'd been trespassing, Laurel moved quickly back to the day room and sat down in front of the typewriter. For the next two hours she busied herself typing a stencil of daily activities and retyping another for church services which she discovered at the back of the desk.

The gong for lunch had just sounded when Casey pushed open the door and pulled up in surprise. "You're still here?"

"I was just leaving. There are the stencils you wanted . . ." she watched him move over to inspect them. "Is everything all right? I wasn't sure which movie you'd scheduled so I guessed." Hesitantly she added, "Are you sure they gave you the right titles?"

"I think so. Why?" He looked up, frowning.

"Well, I don't think anybody's going to stand in line to see *Camille* and *The Birth of a Nation.* Or *Boys' Town* with Mickey Rooney as a juvenile lead. It sounds as if you ordered them from the public library."

"Maybe the front office is saving money on the entertainment budget. Never mind, we'll tell everybody it's a Film Classic series." He picked up another stencil. "Why did you bother typing the church service again?"

"Because 'Holy' which comes before Bible still has only one 'l' in it. You'd put two in your version. You're a terrible speller," she added frankly.

"Damn! I meant to change it. It's a good thing you have hidden assets."

"I'm glad you think so. If that's all . . . I'll be going."

Casey looked over his shoulder, clearly surprised to find her still there. "Sure. I'll expect you tomorrow morning about the same time."

He didn't say "if that's all right with you," Laurel noted with annoyance. Unfortunately, silent indignation was the only thing possible on her part. Casey had already gone into his bedroom and closed the door behind him.

Her bad temper had evaporated after she washed and made her way to the deck luncheon. By the time she selected an appetizing plateful from the buffet table, Rip was waiting for her.

"Mr. Grayson is saving a place for you outside," he informed her. "Said he'd have my head if I didn't bring you along."

"We can't allow that." Laurel paused to select a piece of cake for dessert. "Lead on. I have enough food already to last me for the rest of the week."

Rip pushed open the lounge door with his shoulder. "This is nothing. You should see what some of the passengers eat."

Eduardo rose from his chair at a small table overlooking the pool. "Finally," he greeted her. "I was beginning to think you'd decided to swim back to Long Beach."

"Not a chance." Laurel sat down and nodded her thanks to Rip. "After seeing this food, I may even stow away for the next trip."

"Will you have coffee with your lunch?" Rip asked, still hovering behind her chair.

"Please . . . but there's no hurry."

"I'll bring it right away," he assured her.

She stared after him as he scuttled away. "He must have turned over a new leaf since breakfast."

Eduardo's fork stopped halfway to his mouth. "Why? What happened then?"

"Nothing really vital but he dropped the sugar bowl twice and brought orange juice for dessert."

"That's par for Rip at breakfast." The Brazilian started to gesture and then decided to eat the meat ball on his fork before he dropped it. "Why do you think Peg and I turned up absent."

"I *did* wonder." She smiled at his embarrassed expression. Not that anything disconcerted Eduardo for long, she was discovering. Today he was wearing a navy blue sports outfit that complimented his sleek, dark hair and tanned skin. It fitted the relaxed and luxurious atmosphere aboard ship as neatly as his assured manner.

"I meant to warn you," he was saying. "Have the stewardess bring your breakfast and patronize the deck lunch. That means you only have to cope with Rip for one meal. Saves wear and tear on him, too."

"You may be right." She fell silent as the young waiter brought her coffee and refilled Eduardo's cup.

"Anything else I can do for you?" he wanted to know.

"Not a thing, Rip. We're all set."

"Then I'll see you tonight." The young man gave them both an uncertain smile and went back into the lounge.

"The poor kid's scared. Somebody must have been reading him the riot act," Eduardo commented as he took a sip of coffee.

"Do waiters come under Mr. Waring's department?" Laurel asked, remembering with a guilty pang how she had complained about the slow breakfast service.

"Just indirectly. Rip is officially under the chief steward." Eduardo sounded tired of the subject. "Where have you been all morning?"

"In the chief purser's day room." As his eyebrows went up, she added hastily, "Going steady with a typewriter. Casey wasn't around. He's asked me to help out. They're short of help since the social director cancelled out at the last minute."

Eduardo's dark eyebrows came together in a scowl. "How much time do you have to put in?"

"Only an hour or so in the forenoons. It should be interesting," she admitted. "At least, I'll know the schedule for the day."

"You don't need a job for that. Tonight there's the captain's cocktail party to greet everybody who came aboard in Long Beach. The day after tomorrow, there'll be another party to say good-bye to the passengers getting off at the first port . . ."

"And the next night, we'll have another to meet the passengers getting on in Manzanillo," she finished for him.

"Exactly. You can set your watch by it. Cruise passengers go to cocktail parties the way other people brush their teeth or put the cat out. It gives the women a chance to show off their wardrobe and the men an excuse for . . ." his voice trailed off. "I'll let you find *that* out for yourself."

"It might be safer." She looked at her watch after finishing her last bite of cold turkey and potato salad. "There should be plenty of time for a swim and some sun before the festivities."

He reached in his shirt pocket and found his cigarettes. "I hoped you'd feel like that. May I keep you company?"

"Of course," she said, starting her dessert. "I'd better make an effort to meet some of the other passengers, too."

He lit his cigarette and dropped the match in a deep ashtray. "My dear Laurel . . . you can't escape. The line will form to the right as soon as you put on a swim suit and approach the pool." As she started to protest, he held up a hand. "No . . . don't make polite noises. It's the truth—just wait and see."

A little later, Laurel found that he was right. In the hour or so they spent by the pool, she met fully half of the passenger list.

"And *all* of the men," Eduardo said when she commented on it. "You'd think that a retired judge from Berkeley would have other interests but he was as bad as the real estate salesman from Hollywood."

"I thought they were both nice."

"They had to be. Their wives were on the other side of the pool watching."

Laurel swung her feet to the deck and sat up on her lounge. "You're a cynic, Eduardo."

He stood up beside her and put his shirt on. "You're right. And it's a new feeling for me. I thought I was past the age for competing, but having you around is affecting my blood pressure."

"The way you keep mentioning age makes you sound like Methuselah."

"I'm thirty-seven . . ."

"So?" Her expression was mischievous.

He laughed and reached over to take her chin in his hand. "Right now, I feel about twenty."

"You said that people shed years when they get to sea," she reminded him.

"So we should stay at sea all the time," came a soft, accented voice.

Laurel turned to see the Countess displaying a very nice figure in a black swim suit as she paused beside them.

Eduardo filled in the expectant silence. "Luisa . . . this is Laurel Cavanaugh. Miss Cavanaugh . . . the Countess de Lazlo."

"Luisa, please," the older woman said with a pretty grimace. "The title is Polish and now I'm a citizen of Canada where we have no need for such things." She turned back to Laurel. "Are you enjoying the cruise so far?"

"It's wonderful. The sea is so calm it's unbelievable. I have to pinch myself every now and then to know this is real."

Eduardo put a tanned arm around her shoulders casually. "If you'd told me, I would have been glad to oblige . . ."

The Countess shook her head in mock reproof. "Watch him, Laurel. I've learned that all Brazilian men are dangerous . . . especially the ones who've lived in the States. They seem quiet and polite but . . ."

"They're not." Laurel kept her voice just as solemn. "I'll remember."

"Fine thing," Eduardo complained. "I think I'm insulted."

The Countess tapped him on the forearm with a tapering finger. "You're being complimented. No woman wants a man who's safe." It seemed to Laurel that the older woman hesitated for a long moment before she went on defiantly. "It takes all the fun out of romance. There has to be an element of uncertainty . . . of danger."

Eduardo pretended to frown. "That's a tall order. I only have ten days till Lima," he confessed to Laurel, "but I'll do my best."

Both women burst out laughing at his earnest expression.

"You're dangerous enough now," Laurel assured him. "Any more and I'll have to trade you in for the judge over there."

Luisa's shoulders shook with laughter under the thin straps of her swim suit. "The judge isn't dangerous . . . but I think his wife might be. Now I must go if I'm to look decent at the cocktail party." Her smile encompassed both of them. "See you there."

Laurel watched her pass through the glass doors into the pool deck and reached for her towel on the back of the lounge. "I have to go, too." Then, absently, "She's nice, isn't she?"

Eduardo nodded.

Laurel was staring at the doors. "She doesn't seem the kind . . ."

"For what?" he prompted when her voice trailed off.

"Well, you know what Peg Purcell said." Laurel sounded uncomfortable. "About the Countess and the captain."

Eduardo's shrug was typically Latin. "On a ship, gossip is always thick. Who knows what the truth is? One thing I'm certain . . . Luisa would be discreet."

"And the captain?"

"Most assuredly. He doesn't let affairs of the heart interfere with his position. All the rules will be followed at the cocktail party. You'll see."

"If I don't dry my hair, I won't be presentable enough to go. Thanks for keeping me company this afternoon, Eduardo."

"Laurel . . ." His soft call caught her before she'd taken more than a step away. "You'll go to the party with me?"

She was a little disturbed by his intensity, but didn't let it show in her reply. "Of course. I'll look forward to it. Just knock on my door when you're ready."

"I'll come by about six. We should be on time to go through the receiving line."

"Receiving line!" she made a wry face. "I'm glad you'll be there to give me moral support. I'm not used to such grandeur on shore. No wonder you call this the Never-Never Land."

"You haven't seen anything yet," he promised. "Wait until the party."

As they went up the stairs to the smaller Inca Lounge that evening at a few minutes after six, Laurel was glad she'd put on her prettiest long dress . . . a confection of pale pink chiffon with a wide pleated collar which added a demure note to the slashed bodice and flowing skirt. All around them, other passengers were clad in their best finery, with the women in long dresses and the men looking especially distinguished in dinner jackets.

"Some freighter," Laurel murmured in an undertone as they waited to go through the line. "It's a good thing I packed some dressy things at the last minute."

Eduardo grinned down at her, looking immaculate in his midnight blue dinner jacket. "A cargo liner is not a freighter when it comes to clothes."

"You can say that again. I've seen shabbier turn-outs at the opera." She peered around the couple in front of them as the line moved forward. "Do all the officers attend these?"

"No . . . just the top ones. After all, somebody still has to run the ship."

"That did occur to me," she told him in an

aside as they swept forward into the crowded lounge. They were promptly ushered to the formal line of ship's officers who were dressed in impressive white mess jackets trimmed in gold above black trousers.

"Miss Cavanaugh? I'm Ted Jensen, the chief officer." A pleasant bald-headed man in his forties shook hands with her. "Nice to have you with us. May I present Captain Samuels." He passed her along smoothly to a tall middle-aged man whose thinning dark hair was streaked with gray at the temples. His broad shoulders were impressive in his formal uniform and he held himself with authority. After one look, Laurel suspected that the polite welcome on his tanned countenance was generated for the occasion.

"Miss Cavanaugh . . . I'm happy to meet you. Casey was saying how you'd volunteered to help since we're shorthanded." He smiled down at her in avuncular fashion. "Don't let him work you too hard."

The only possible reply was an equally meaningless cliché, Laurel thought to herself, and hoped his conversation improved when he was talking to the Countess. Aloud, she murmured that she certainly wasn't being overworked and was enjoying the trip immensely.

"Good, good," he boomed promptly although by then his glance had slid over her shoulder to Eduardo. "Nothing like a happy ship, eh, Grayson?"

Laurel took her cue and moved on down the line, shaking hands with the chief steward who had owl-like glasses, a receding forehead, and a harassed expression undoubtedly put there by some of his waiters. Beyond him, there was a stolid-looking chief engineer who looked as if his ancestors worked the Black Sea or Murmansk run. Then she found herself face to face with Casey Waring who didn't shake hands but bowed with exaggerated politeness. "Miss Cavanaugh . . ." There was an undercurrent of laughter in his tone. "So glad you were able to make it."

His words were cut off abruptly by Eduardo's comment as he came up behind Laurel. "Good God, Casey . . . what did you do to yourself?"

"What d'you mean?" The chief purser flushed slightly as he turned to shake hands with him.

"That fringe on your upper lip. I thought you were devoted to it. Now, here you are . . . the soul of respectability again. There must be a reason." Eduardo's features took on a knowing look. "Is she aboard yet or coming on at Manzanillo?"

"If you think I'm telling, you're crazy," Casey said in an undertone.

Laurel found herself marveling at his appearance along with Eduardo. Not only had the moustache gone, his hair was neatly brushed, and his starched shirt and uniform jacket were tailored by a master hand. Whoever had effected the change was a force to be reckoned with.

Evidently Eduardo was thinking the same thing. "Never mind," he told Casey, taking Laurel's elbow to move her along, "I'll find out eventually. Nothing's sacred at sea. You should know by now."

Casey just gave him a mocking smile. "I appreciate your taking such care of my new assistant. See you later when this line breaks up."

After Eduardo had commandeered a waiter,

gotten their drinks, and refused two trays of canapés, he was able to steer Laurel into a fairly deserted corner. "Now, if you'll stay close beside me and appear fascinated by what I'm saying, we may discourage anyone from joining us."

She giggled. "You *are* unsociable. I thought we were supposed to mingle."

"Why? We'll see these same people morning, noon, and night for the next ten days. There's no point in using up all our conversation at the very beginning." He stiffened as he felt a hand on his shoulder and Laurel had trouble keeping a straight face at his annoyed expression.

"There's no point in turning your back, Eduardo. I'm not going away." Peg Purcell, resplendent in an aqua sequined gown surveyed them calmly. "George is still making his apologies to the captain. He was supposed to be in the line, but we came late," she explained to Laurel and then beckoned to a red-faced officer with thinning gray hair.

Aside from his heightened complexion color, the doctor was of average appearance. Just then, his full face bore an exasperated expression and his glance moved around the room nervously as he approached. "Damn it, Peg. You should have wakened me," he said, pulling up beside them. "The captain's madder than hell." He broke off to survey Laurel with obvious approval.

His wife interrupted his appraisal. "Stop fussing, George. Laurel—this is my husband . . . as you undoubtedly gathered."

"How do you do, Dr. Purcell."

He took her literally. "Better tonight, thanks. Sorry I wasn't around to greet you in Long Beach, but we can make up for it. Eduardo—*como está*?"

"Bem, obrigado." The other raised his glass. "You'd better catch up with us."

"The captain will kill me if I do. I've had the word to circulate." Dr. Purcell urged his wife toward the middle of the room as he said, "Nice to have met you, Laurel. Don't let Eduardo monopolize you. The judge looks as if he's headed this way . . ." He grinned at her stricken expression. "Don't worry, Peg and I'll run interference for you. After all this time, we're good at it. See you two at dinner."

Laurel sighed with relief as she saw the Purcells move across to intercept the judge and his wife by the piano.

"I'd have preferred the judge to some of those vultures," Eduardo said, jerking his head toward the officers in the now-disbanding receiving line. "The chief engineer has been ogling you for the last five minutes."

Laurel watched a striking redhead cross the engineer's path and start a conversation. "Too bad. I'll never survive that competition. Isn't she the actress who was at the captain's table?"

He nodded. "Gwen Harper. She must be killing time. The chief isn't her type."

Before Laurel could ask who was, a familiar figure pulled up beside them. "Captain Samuels told me to take care of 'the young lady from the advertising department' and 'our biggest freight customer,' " Casey Waring reported. "That's why I'm here. Anything I can do to make you two happy? More ice cubes . . . another crock of caviar? The captain's wish is my command."

"I don't think he said anything of the sort," Laurel commented with sudden suspicion.

Casey put up his hand. "Scout's honor. Those are the orders from the bridge. We have different ones every time we change the watch."

"Every time?" she asked, not sure if he were serious.

"Absolutely. Last night, they said:

'When in question or in doubt
Always keep a good lookout.' "

Eduardo burst out laughing at the expression on Laurel's face. "She really thought you meant it," he told Casey.

"I should have known better," Laurel said. "I suppose there are others?"

"Certainly. The commodore of the fleet framed his over the radar screen:

'Full speed ahead over the bar
How I wonder where we are . . .' "

Casey shook his head when Laurel would have interrupted. "Wait for it—there's a second stanza.

'Back her, stop her, turn around
Pray to God she's not aground.' "

Laurel started to giggle despite herself.

"And you haven't heard the one Captain Samuels has over his bed." He waited for her to shake her head and went on impressively, "It's called the 'first rule of command' on the *Ocean Traveler.*"

"Tell me, Mr. Bones," she said just as solemnly, "what is the first rule of command on this ship?"

Casey quoted obediently,

" 'When in danger or in doubt
Run in circles, scream and shout.' "

Then, as Laurel shook her head in despair, he grinned and went on in a normal tone. "Don't worry, there's no need to put on your life jacket. The second and third mates are conscientious young men and good at their jobs."

"I don't see them here tonight," she said, looking around.

"And you won't . . . ever," Casey replied firmly. "Somebody has to tend the store and the chief officer does all the socializing for the navigation staff. Plus the captain, of course." He broke off as the chief officer came toward them. "I wonder what Ted Jensen wants."

The first mate didn't keep them in doubt for long. "Sorry to interrupt this," he said in his calm, pleasant manner, "but there's a man on the other side of the room who wants to talk to you, Eduardo. He's going to Rio next month and has some questions." He turned to Laurel. "I promise to return him in good time."

"Make damned sure you do," Eduardo growled. "I won't be long, Laurel. See that you behave yourself, Casey," he added before trailing the chief officer over to the other side of the crowded lounge.

Laurel raised her eyebrows. "That . . . from an old friend? What a reputation you've gathered, Mr. Waring."

"I suggest we both forget it." Casey took out an immaculate handkerchief and mopped his brow. "Let's go outside for a breather," he said, jerking his head toward the doors leading to the afterdeck. "It's hotter than the fringes of hell in here. The air-conditioning must have gone off again."

Laurel wasn't disposed to argue. The temperature in the crowded room had suddenly shot up, making her clothes feel as if they'd been glued to her.

They made their way slowly across the room. Casey nodded and responded to greetings from either side, but he didn't pause in his move toward the door. Once outside, he led the way to an isolated corner of the deck and leaned against the railing.

"Too much breeze for your hair?" he asked.

"No—it feels good." She gave a sigh of satisfaction. "I think I'll stay out here. Cocktail parties aren't my favorite entertainment. When you go back, would you tell Eduardo where I am, please?"

"Don't be in such a hurry to get rid of me. Eduardo will survive the separation. I'm not so sure about you. Better not take him seriously."

Laurel's lips thinned in protest. "You don't have to play the heavy father with me . . . I can take care of myself. Why don't you spend your time warning the Countess in there." Her head moved toward the lounge where the figures of the captain and Luisa huddled in earnest conversation. Even from that distance, they could see that the older woman was sparkling vivaciously and that the captain was basking in her approval—his former indifference a thing of the past.

"Maybe you should speak to both of them," Laurel said bitterly. "After all, they're married, aren't they?"

"Very much so. Unfortunately not to each other."

"And old enough to know better," Laurel taunted.

Casey frowned. "Don't be so quick to condemn. People live when they're at sea, too. You can't put your feelings in cold storage until you tie up again at the Long Beach pier."

"That's an old refrain," Laurel murmured disdainfully.

"Evidently the captain believes it," Casey said. "He was telling me the other day that he'd met six women in his life with whom he could have been equally happy."

"I hope he has the good sense not to mention it to his wife or the Countess."

"You don't approve?" There was laughter under his tone.

Laurel smoothed her chiffon collar and discovered her fingers were trembling with anger. "I don't like sharing," she told him flatly. "I never have. When I was in fifth grade, there was a boy who bragged that he received fourteen valentines besides mine."

"What did you do?"

"I took mine off his desk and tore it up."

Casey was watching her closely. "You should have torn up the other fourteen. Where's your spirit of competition?"

"Long gone. I refuse to stand in line for favors." For some reason, it seemed important that Laurel get her point across. "When a man wants me, he'll have to give up any ideas for a harem."

"Quality instead of quantity." He was mocking her openly.

"Something like that." She stared at him defiantly. "You don't approve?"

"I'm a bachelor . . . that puts me in a different category from the captain," he pointed out. "I have no intention of getting married for another five years at least. I make that plain to women at the beginning. Once the ground rules are announced, there can't be any hurt feelings later. It works very well." As he noted her skeptical expression, he looked amused. "Not with you, I see."

"It isn't for me to say," she replied stiffly, "but I'm surprised that some woman hasn't gone after you with a razor before this. How in the world did we ever get on this subject?"

"You took exception when I said that falling in love is Standard Operating Procedure for a woman on a cruise. A little romance is good for everybody . . . sort of a therapy."

"Therapy!" Laurel's strained tone gave away more than she intended but she couldn't help it. "I've never heard such drivel! You've either been at sea too long or you're an anachronism and you belong back with the dinosaurs."

Gwen Harris swept out beside them in time to hear the last. "Not my Casey," she said, twining a shapely tanned arm through his uniform sleeve. "I want him here right next to me."

Casey's expression was impassive but he didn't disengage his arm. Laurel could only hope that he'd choke on the fumes of Chanel #5 which were suddenly engulfing them. Just because the woman wore gorgeous clothes and had a striking figure to display them was no reason for the chief purser to look at her with that disgusting expression.

Casey saw her disdain and his look of amusement deepened. "Laurel Cavanaugh . . . Gwen Harper. Miss Harper's sailed with us on the *Traveler* before."

He needn't have explained, Laurel thought bitterly. From the way the redhead was still gazing soulfully up at him, it was obvious they were well acquainted.

"I'm happy to know you, Miss Harper," Laurel managed to say, belatedly remembering her job. Marden Steam didn't like its passengers insulted—no matter what the provocation. "If you'll excuse me, I'd better find Eduardo."

"Don't worry, honey, we can send him out to you when the gong rings," Gwen said. She tugged gently at Casey, "I thought you were going to have a drink with me. You practically promised."

"There's still time. You go ahead." He paused to give Laurel an amused look before following the redhead. "I enjoyed our discussion." When Laurel remained stubbornly silent, he added softly, "I hope you'll remember what I said. It might help for the rest of the voyage."

Her chin went up. Apparently he'd chosen to disregard her views—his were the only ones that mattered. "Your . . . friend . . . is waiting, Mr. Waring," she reminded.

"No doubt. Are you going to the movie tonight?"

"I think not." She matched his insouciance. "Garbo in *Camille* sounds too much like the Swing Shift Movie on TV. I'll wash out a few things and go to bed. Alone."

"Of that I had no doubt. I'll see you at ten in the morning."

"Casey, darling . . ." Gwen Harper's throaty voice sounded annoyed.

For the first time, so did he. "I'm coming." Despite his unruffled exterior, the short-tempered retort was familiar. He gave Laurel a last irritable look and strode back into the crowded lounge.

Her aloof expression faded as he disappeared through the doors. Why was it that every time she exchanged more than one sentence with the man she felt as if she'd been thrown into the turbulence of the ship's propellers. It was too bad that she hadn't been warned before she left home.

Her chief at the San Francisco branch had merely said, "Keep your eyes open while you're away. You may pick up some pointers!" He didn't mention the danger of encountering a man like Casey Waring who treated a woman's emotions like a sack of cargo destined for the hold.

Laurel shook her head as she went over to stare down at the black waters surging past the *Traveler*'s sides. The situation made her recall the words of a visiting Russian orchestra conductor when he took a first look at a difficult score. "Some is easy," he had said. "Some is uneasy."

Without a doubt, Casey Waring fitted in the latter category.

Chapter Three

The next morning when Laurel reported for work at the chief purser's day room, she found Casey lounging in his comfortable chair under the porthole, long legs stretched out in front of him.

"Things are improving," he said. "You're almost on time."

"So is the breakfast service." She pretended to look around. "No stopwatch? You're slipping, Mr. Waring."

"I've had enough of being 'Mr. Waring.' You can drop the formality any time." He stared at her quizzically. "Somebody should have whittled you down to size before this. Or beaten you regularly . . . twice a day. Would've saved me the trouble."

"Well, I like that!"

"The hell you do." He grinned amiably as he stood up. "Okay, I apologize. No offense meant. I like to watch your eyes flash when you get mad. I like your outfit, too."

"Oh . . . this." Since she'd spent the better part of ten minutes deciding what to wear before settling on a bibbed pinafore in blue and white chambray worn with a French-type workshirt, Laurel's casual response was definitely suspect.

Casey's narrowed eyes made her realize it. Her cheeks reddened as his masculine glance went over her once again and she sat down hastily in front of the typewriter to cover her confusion.

"How's Eduardo this morning?" Casey asked pleasantly.

"I couldn't say ... he breakfasts in his cabin. I decided to take my chances with Rip in the dining room again. How's Miss Harper?"

He copied her tone faithfully. "I couldn't say. I settled for the officers' mess. Now—are we even?"

She looked up and met his amused grin with one of her own. "I think so. I'll sheathe my claws. Oh—I meant to tell you—I've solved one of your problems. About the missing pillowcases ..."

He relaxed visibly. "What's the story?"

"You'll never believe it. I found out from Hal this morning. He discovered that the new steward on the other corridor ..."

"The one called Flash?"

She nodded. "Well, it seems Flash decided to save himself some work, so he put six pillowcases on each pillow in his staterooms. His idea was that each time he changed the linen, he'd just peel off the outer case."

"My God!"

She laughed at Casey's stricken face. "Be thankful that he didn't decide to do the same thing with the sheets."

"If Flash lets the ship get back in one piece, I'll be surprised. You wouldn't believe the things he's done so far."

"Maybe one of our competitors smuggled him aboard."

"Very possibly." He watched her scan the notes for the Good Morning sheet he'd left by the typewriter. "Any questions about that?"

"Not really. I see Peg Purcell is taking the exercise class this morning."

"And the craft class this afternoon. She decided the women would like to make eyeglass cases. I hope she's right." Casey didn't sound very convinced.

"What about this bridge tournament?" Laurel was down to the afternoon schedule. "Who runs it?"

The chief purser ran a finger around his shirt collar as if it had suddenly shrunk. "I meant to ask you about that. You *do* play bridge?" When she nodded reluctantly, he went on. "All you have to do is check the scores and supply the cards. Everything's in the desk drawer on the left." He started for the door. "Well, I'd better get to work . . ."

"Don't run away," she told him tartly. "You're sure that I'm not responsible for the lifeboat drill after that or the gala dance after dinner?"

He paused with his hand on the knob and gave her a mocking look. "Not unless you want to volunteer. The dance is 'ladies choice.' Shall I save you a place on my program?"

"You'd better wait and see if there are any holes."

"I'll make one . . ."

"Between the Countess and Miss Harper." Despite herself, there was an edge to her voice.

"I was thinking of the last waltz, but whatever you prefer."

She pulled out a stencil and banged the desk drawer shut. "I'd hate to get trampled in the crowd. If anyone calls, what shall I tell them?"

"Whatever you want. Don't forget that you'll be busy when we get in Manzanillo tomorrow." His tone lost all traces of humor. "I can use your help on the tour bus."

"What about Eduardo?"

"He'll have to get along without you. Everybody makes sacrifices now and then."

That made her angry enough to argue. "And what about you? What are you going to be doing?"

"Checking with the Marden representative there and making sure that a very important passenger gets aboard. Any more questions?"

She would have liked to find out who that important passenger was but knew better than to ask. "No . . . that's all . . . Mr. Waring."

"Casey . . ." he snapped with an annoyed look.

"Casey."

It was hard for her to get the name out and he must have known it because his eyes narrowed. "It'll come easier after you've said it a few times. See you later."

The morning went quickly after that. Word must have gotten around that Casey was working elsewhere because the telephone by Laurel's elbow seldom rang. She had just finished her typing jobs when she heard the luncheon gong and she made her way to the deck lunch without seeing the chief purser again.

Evidently Laurel wasn't the only one who wondered where he'd gone. As she shared a table with

Eduardo and Peg Purcell, she saw Gwen Harper looking up anxiously each time a uniformed man came through the lounge doors. When Casey hadn't appeared by dessert, the actress moved to join the Countess after the older woman announced that she was going down by the pool to get some sun.

"There go our social leaders," Peg said when the two women trailed down the outside stairs. "I didn't think they'd attend my crafts class. Not that I hold it against them. They're showing good sense."

"Why is that?" Eduardo wanted to know.

"I think something's wrong with my pattern for the afternoon's project." Peg rummaged in a tote bag and pulled out an oddly shaped creation. "This was my trial run," she confessed. "George says it looks more like a distended appendix than an eyeglass case."

Eduardo was convulsed with laughter. "Your husband's being charitable. I think it's a cover for small hot-water bottles."

"How about an all-purpose bag?" Laurel said helpfully, taking pity on Peg's stricken countenance. "Who's to know?"

"Only Casey," the blond woman admitted. "And I could kill him for getting me into this in the first place. What are *you* doing this afternoon?" she asked Laurel with sudden suspicion.

"Running the bridge tournament."

"Assisted by me," Eduardo concluded.

It was the first Laurel had heard of it, but she shot him a grateful look. "I need all the help I can get."

"Which means I'm on my own," Peg grumbled.

Eduardo folded his napkin and put it on the table. "Not at all. If you have trouble with the women, just refer them to Casey."

"He doesn't know anything about teaching crafts."

"There are other ways of soothing irate passengers and Casey is an expert on that," he said getting up. "We'd better get the cards and things," he told Laurel. "Bridge players have no sense of humor if they're kept waiting."

She nodded as she stood up to join him.

"Remember to finish your tournament before the lifeboat drill," Peg put in. "Captain Samuels takes that seriously, too."

Eduardo waved a hand. "We'll be on time, even if it means missing a slam bid . . . a small slam, that is."

When the clanging of the ship's alarm bell was heard two hours later, the first session of the bridge tournament had been safely concluded. Laurel was relieved that all the players were still in a good humor with the possible exception of the judge's wife who'd gone down five tricks vulnerable on the last hand.

"She can't blame anybody but herself," Eduardo reassured Laurel as they picked up their life jackets and made for the main lounge. "Her partner did everything except pitch a fit on the floor to shut her up."

"Well, I appreciated your help," Laurel said gratefully as they followed the other passengers down the stairs and into the main lounge. "Do we put these on now?" She started to loosen the straps on the bulky orange jacket.

An announcement came just then from the speaker over their heads. "Passengers will don their life jackets when they reach their muster station. In case of a real emergency, passengers should bring a blanket with them and a coat for use in lifeboats." The gong sounded again, followed by the terse announcement, "Crew members . . . assemble at their stations."

"Look at everybody! I had no idea they'd take this so seriously," Laurel said in a light tone to Eduardo who was getting into his life jacket behind her. Unfortunately, Casey heard her as he came through the door, looking solidly official in his life jacket, with his uniform cap at a no-nonsense angle on his head.

"You're damned right we take it seriously," he told her in an undertone meant for her ears alone. "So does the U. S. Coast Guard."

"I . . . I didn't mean . . ." Her words fizzled under his level glance. "Oh, help . . . I'm sorry."

He nodded as if he didn't have any more time to waste and then he passed on up the line, patiently spelling out the procedure for an actual emergency to the passengers and showing them how to file out to the boats on deck if the occasion arose. A few minutes later, he repeated his announcement in Spanish for their Mexican and South American passengers. The emergency gong sounded a final time over their heads with the voice of Captain Samuels coming on immediately afterwards. "This concludes the drill . . . this concludes the drill. Passengers and crew are dismissed. Thank you very much."

Casey didn't need to translate further. The passengers broke into a pleased hum of conversation as they untied their bulky life jackets and shed them.

Casey held up a hand before they could leave the lounge. "One last thing ... if any passengers are missing whistles on their life jackets, please let Miss Cavanaugh know. She's hiding over there by the pillar. Laurel—make a list of their staterooms," he called to her. "We'll deliver the missing merchandise this afternoon."

"Skip the whistle . . . I'll settle for Miss Cavanaugh," said a masculine voice from the back of the lounge and the rest of the passengers broke into a roar of delighted laughter.

Casey grinned as well. "Sorry. We're not giving her away so early on the cruise. Remember, when you're at sea, it's a seller's market and I imagine the lady has other plans." He waited for a moment and then went on with a look of devilment. "I know I have."

"Honestly!" Laurel seethed as she watched him disappear in the midst of a jovial group of passengers. She turned to Eduardo. "That man gets away with murder. He made me sound like one of the door prizes for the Christmas costume party." Then as she saw his amused expression, she smiled reluctantly. "Don't you dare suggest it to him!"

"I'll try to restrain myself. It may take most of the dances tonight for you to persuade me. Now let's get rid of these life jackets and enjoy ourselves for the rest of the day."

The next morning, Laurel hurried through her breakfast so that she could go on deck and watch the Mexican shoreline as the *Traveler* approached the port of Manzanillo. For once, she and Rip shared a common desire and he set a new speed record in bringing her omelet and coffee.

Once she had finished, she made her way up to the flying bridge she had discovered the first night aboard. She was delighted to find it apparently deserted as she climbed the last steps to the glassed-in platform and hesitated in disappointment when she noticed a tall, broad-shouldered figure standing on the far side.

When he turned slowly to acknowledge her presence, the chief purser's face didn't give anything away either. "Good morning, Laurel."

"I didn't know you'd be here," she stammered before he could say more. "I just meant to see what was happening before I went down and started work."

"Don't make me sound like such a taskmaster! I think we both showed remarkable sense. It's a beautiful morning, and I, for one, can use some fresh air."

She scrutinized him closely. "You do look a little tired . . ."

"There's no need to be diplomatic. I also have a monumental hangover which came from introducing Pisco Sours to half the passenger list last night. Piscos are the national drink in Peru," he explained, "and everybody felt a preview was indicated."

"I see." Laurel went over to lean against the railing. Just then, her mind wasn't on the Mexican coastline which showed gray and purple tinges as the morning sun accentuated the foothills at the water's edge and the higher mountain range behind them. "I'm surprised that it wasn't tequila in honor of our arrival here."

"Gwen thought tequila was too tame."

Laurel kept her gaze straight ahead, affording him only a disapproving profile. "Miss Harper kept you busy most of the time."

"Was that why you didn't come over for a dance?"

She turned then. "I told you that I didn't stand in line for such things. I meant it."

His voice was softly insinuating. "Even when it's 'ladies choice'?"

"Especially not then." Laurel had no intention of revealing how annoyed she'd been the night before. Although she had to admit that Casey cheerfully abandoned the actress to dance with other women whenever they'd gone over to claim him.

"It was handy that Eduardo saved you the trouble." Waring's tone was offhand and he turned back to rest his elbows on the rail. "Is this your first visit to Manzanillo?" he went on, apparently intent on changing the subject.

She nodded eagerly. "I'm anxious to see it."

"Well, it won't be long now. We tie up at the new pier which is just around that headland there."

"Will we stay very long?"

"About four hours . . . we're due to pick up some cargo here and unload that farm machinery on deck. Your tour bus will be waiting when we dock. I've scheduled a three-hour jaunt around town."

"What about lunch?"

His shoulders shook as he chuckled. "Damned if

you don't sound like a typical cruise passenger. It didn't take you long."

"Isn't it the truth!" Her expression was rueful. "And I just finished breakfast. It must be the salt air or the wonderful luxury of not having to do the dishes."

"I know. Believe me, it takes willpower to keep the calories under control. But getting back to the tour—I've arranged with the chief steward for box lunches on the bus. Be sure and count them to tally with the nose count before you start or there'll be a mutiny en route. The list of names is on the desk next to your typewriter." He looked at his watch and then stifled a yawn. "I'd better get to work or I'll fall asleep here at the rail."

"What's scheduled for tonight after we sail?"

"Another movie."

She winced. "What is it this time?"

"Would you believe *The Jazz Singer*?"

"Nobody will want to go to that," she felt bound to say.

"Then they'll have an excuse for going to bed early, which they'll want to do anyway after a day ashore. If there was a red-hot movie, they'd be madder than hell. This way—everybody's happy."

"And the midnight buffet will again be served at nine thirty?"

"Tonight we can safely advance it to nine o'clock. Hot milk will take the place of coffee."

She started to laugh. "Now I know where they got that phrase . . . 'a restful sea voyage.' "

"Well, for God's sake—don't tell the advertising department. The passengers don't want to be reminded of reality." He started to turn away and then swung back. "I meant to tell you—I could use your help for the Christmas Eve festivities."

"That's only two days from now."

"I know." Casey's growl showed that, despite his hangover, he could still read a calendar. "We'll be tying up at Acajutla that night. It's the port city for El Salvador."

Laurel nearly said that she'd read the itinerary too, but the set of his jaw made her change her mind. "What can I do to help?" she asked meekly.

"Usually we have a midnight church service in the small lounge. I've lined up a pianist for the carols but we'll have to recruit somebody to read the Christmas story. Incidentally, we'll need a stencil for the order of service."

"I'm already ahead of you."

He looked amused at her resigned tone. "Well, it's your own fault for being able to spell. Too bad you don't need a steady job." His attention was caught by a small cruiser which was cutting through the water toward them. "There's the pilot coming aboard—I'd better get below. Remember to take a hat for the sun—it can be hot down here. And watch what you eat ashore."

Her eyes brimmed with mischief. "Shall I tie a peso in my handkerchief for an emergency phone call?"

"It's easy to see you haven't been to Manzanillo before," was his cryptic reply. He reached out to flick a finger under her chin and was gone.

Laurel smiled and turned back to the fascinating business of watching the pilot boat circle before coming alongside as the *Traveler* dropped her speed to remain almost stationary in the water.

The sound of footsteps made her turn to see Dr. Purcell coming up the steps. Today he was immaculate in his starched whites.

"Morning, Laurel," he said in a cheerful tone. "Casey said you were up here."

"I decided they might need help navigating. This was the closest I could come to back-seat driving."

"It never hurts to have plenty of people minding the store," he agreed solemnly. "If you don't approve of the course, you can lean over the rail and remind the captain. He's on the starboard bridge right now."

Laurel grinned back at him, liking his sense of humor. In the morning sunlight, the puffy lines around his eyes were more evident than at the cocktail party, but his florid complexion was considerably subdued after a night's rest.

"I suspect that if I gave any instructions," she told him, "Captain Samuels would have my baggage on the pier when we hit Manzanillo. It'd be my last appearance on the *Traveler*."

"You're right about that. Sailors are notoriously hard-headed." He squinted down into the green water which was swirling around the pilot craft as it maneuvered to allow the pilot aboard. Then he gave a grunt of satisfaction as the lithe Mexican accomplished the transfer.

"He made it," Laurel said with relief.

"What's that?" George Purcell stared blankly at her and then he nodded. "Sure—nothing to it in a sea like this. Now in Lima, we're apt to have some weather."

"You make it sound so easy. I don't think I could ever be casual about it."

"You forget, I've been to sea for a long time. Ever since I sold my practice in New York." He was staring straight ahead, his tone level and without expression. "God knows how I'm going to get used to staying ashore . . . I think I'll have to stow away now and then." The last was said with a wry twist.

"I don't understand."

He turned to face her. "I thought you knew. This is my last trip for Marden. I presumed Casey had told you."

"No. He didn't say a word about it." Somehow it seemed important to make that clear. The doctor was obviously unhappy about leaving the ship, but it was hard to make polite conversation when she didn't know whether he was giving up his job voluntarily or whether Marden had requested it.

He sensed her confusion. "It was a gentleman's agreement," he said, keeping his tone light. "We parted friends. The company's probably right about a shore job—I'm getting a little old for this responsibility."

"Do you have many patients when you're at sea?"

He nodded. "It's not surprising when you consider the age of the passengers. Then there are accidents among the crew plus the other ships without medical facilities. A ship's doctor has his work cut out."

"I hadn't realized . . ."

"Neither did my wife," he said somewhat bitterly. "Peg thought I'd have more free time."

The throbbing of the ship's engines showed that they had started to cleave through the water again and the new signal flag at the mast indicated officially that they had a "Pilot Aboard."

Dr. Purcell looked around and nodded with satsifaction. "It won't be long now. We should be docked in about forty-five minutes."

"Will you be taking the bus tour?" she asked hesitantly, unsure of whether ship's officers had shore leave.

"Not this time. Peg's going along though. I have to see a friend of mine at the local hospital. Had to put a crew member ashore here on the last trip. Thank God there've been no emergencies this time. Getting more linen aboard is our biggest problem."

"That's halfway to being solved," she said, and proceeded to tell him the saga of the missing pillowcases.

"Good lord, no wonder Casey's looking pale around the gills these days," he said when she'd finished. "He'll be old before his time at this rate."

"Especially if he stays on a steady diet of Pisco Sours," she said tartly. "That's what's wrong with him this morning. It serves him right after last night."

The doctor was watching her with interest. "He doesn't make a career of it. Drinking, I mean," he explained when her head came up questioningly. "And I should know—I'm an expert on the topic." He changed the subject before she could comment. "There's the harbor where we dock." He pointed to a pier in the distance as they slid through the opening in the breakwater.

Buildings in the port city were terraced up the hillsides although builders had left plenty of space for luxuriant greenery around the dwellings. Even at that distance, the bougainvillea foliage was brilliant against the landscape while the towering coco palms at the water's edge added a lush tropical touch. Overhead, a thin cloud layer diffused the sun's rays although Laurel felt that it would get much warmer as the day progressed.

The doctor confirmed her suspicions. "They tell a story about this place. When a native of Manzanillo dies and goes down to hell, the first thing he asks for is a blanket. Can't stand the change in temperature."

"I'm beginning to believe it. I hope the bus is air-conditioned."

"It'll be air-conditioned," he told her, "but whether the air-conditioning will be working is another story. Better lock your valuables away before you leave the ship."

"I will. Tell Peg I'll see her on the bus."

He nodded absently and she left him still staring into the slow-moving currents of the bay as the *Traveler* made her way in stately fashion toward the dock.

When the big ship was finally berthed, Laurel followed the other passengers down the gangway to a crowded dock. Some of the Mexicans were already busy on forklifts unloading cargo from the hatches amidship while others waited for the Gantry-type cranes aboard the ship to start moving the container cargo. In addition, there were the sidewalk superintendents who functioned in the same fashion the world over. The Manzanillo brigade lounged in the shade of empty railroad cars on the pier sidings watching the activity.

An attractive Mexican lady who was standing by the tour bus noted Laurel staring at the men.

"Here we have many people and not many jobs," she said in lightly accented English. "And there's not much excitement . . . so the men come down to watch the ships come in." She gestured toward the list in Laurel's hand. "You must be Miss Cavanaugh . . . Casey said you'd be along."

"I didn't know he'd been ashore . . ."

"I went aboard with the immigration officials when you first docked." Her dark eyes sparkled. "Although I don't worry about our tours when Casey handles things."

So Mr. Waring had another admirer, Laurie thought with some derision. The list was beginning to achieve epidemic proportions. "I'm surprised that he ever took a shore job," she commented lightly.

The other woman shrugged. "Like most men, I suppose he got bored with the routine. Now, I'll get your passengers seated," she said with a return to her businesslike air. "You can check them off when they're aboard. Ah," she added with satisfaction, "here come the lunches . . . right on time."

As the Manzanillo tour progressed, Laurel soon found that she had little to do other than finish her own lunch, chat with the passengers, and thoroughly enjoy the scenery at the sleepy port city. The tour bus drove through the city park with its plantings of mango trees and palms plus a special section devoted to topiary. The boxwood animals emerged just as professionally clipped as those in old English formal gardens. Later the bus driver headed out of town past papaya and banana plantations and finally an extensive orchard of citrus fruit. A lagoon at the orchard's edge was alive with white herons and spoonbills who frolicked in the calm, deep blue waters.

The last stop on the tour was a luxury hotel on the far side of the bay. Laurel was amused to find the hotel's architecture was straight from Babylon with rounded Byzantine roofs on the white stucco buildings and gardens that looked as if they'd been transported from Morocco. When the passengers later walked into the lobby and found a convention of American refrigerator salesmen consuming tortillas at a groaning buffet table, Laurel shook her head and decided to try the gift shop in the annex.

There she found a gum-chewing clerk bent over a showcase as she selected a box of cigars for Casey Waring. The chief purser was accompanied by an attractive young brunette whose gleaming straight hair reached almost to her waist. The girl was in her late teens but boasted a voluptuous figure that didn't have anything of the schoolgirl about it.

Peg Purcell came over to stand beside Laurel in the gift shop doorway. "I'll hand it to Casey," she said. "He does know how to pick them."

"He's old enough to be that one's father," Laurel said acidly. "Let's go back to the hotel lobby, shall we?"

"Don't be in such a hurry. Casey's beckoning us over. Come on, we're blocking traffic here," the doctor's wife said, taking Laurel's elbow and pulling her along like a reluctant relative. "Hi, Casey—I didn't think we'd see you here."

He didn't rise to that. Instead he simply said, "There's someone I want you to meet. May I present Senorita Elena Sanchez . . . Miss Cavanaugh . . . Mrs. Purcell." As they murmured politely, he went on, "Elena's sailing to Lima with us on this trip."

"That sounds like a nice holiday for you," Laurel told the girl pleasantly.

Elena shrugged. "I was having a nice holiday *here*. Too nice. That's why my parents ordered me to join them. Casey has to watch over me." Her dark eyes gleamed. "I think he'd like to dump me in the hold."

"That's where you'll end up if you don't behave yourself," he promised. "Come on, *chica* . . . make up your mind. Are you buying those cigars for your father or not?"

Laurel watched as Elena directed her attention back to the display case. In a short sleeveless white dress with a square neckline, the girl's tanned skin was strikingly lovely. When you added pert features and sloe-black eyes, she made every other woman in the room feel like a jaded hag.

Laurel managed to keep from smoothing her own hair and deliberately avoided a mirror which showed that her lipstick was a thing of the past. "If you'll excuse me," she kept her voice cheerful as she addressed the chief purser's back, "I think I'd better get back with the others."

He swung around, surprised to still find her there. "You're right. The bus should be leaving any time. Peg's already on the sidewalk."

"Will you and Miss Sanchez be joining us?" Laurel asked, refusing to be stampeded.

Elena looked around to say, "*Dios* . . . no! We have our own car and driver."

"Then I won't ask our driver to wait for you," Laurel said, keeping her temper under control. "I'll see you aboard the ship."

"Oh, Laurel . . ." Casey's call caught her halfway to the shop door. "Any problems on the tour so far?"

"Not really. One lady didn't like her sandwiches for lunch but traded them with the bus driver for his oranges. The judge's wife wanted to buy two lovebirds in a cage from a man who was selling them in the park."

"Damnation . . . she can't do that."

"That's what I told her. She was going to argue until I said the poor birds would be seasick for the rest of the trip."

His dark eyebrows came together. "Where did you hear that?"

"I didn't." She went on defiantly. "But nobody knew enough to argue with me, so we drove on."

Casey grinned slowly. "No doubt about it . . . you're a genius."

She managed to keep her tone light. "The bird seller didn't think so. You should have heard the string of Spanish that floated in the bus window when we started off."

Elena looked up, interested for the first time. "Maybe I would have learned something, Casey."

"I doubt it. You know enough four-letter words now to make a longshoreman hang his head. You could be giving lessons instead of taking them."

"I'm pretty damn good in English, too," Elena reported.

Laurel decided to leave before she heard any more home truths.

Peg was waiting impatiently by the bus. "Everybody's aboard," she hissed, "and madder than you-know-what because they had to wait."

Laurel grimaced. "Casey called me back . . ."

"That's no excuse. Get on the bus, but look sick."

"Do *what*?"

Peg paused with her foot on the bus step. "I told them that you had a touch of 'Montezuma's Revenge.' "

Laurel's eyes widened. "Thanks a lot," she got out finally.

"Well, it was the only thing I could think of on the spur of the moment," Peg said in an undertone. "Besides, it worked fine. Everybody feels sorry for you and we can go straight back to the ship without any more stops. We're missing a museum at the edge of town but nobody wanted to see it anyhow." With that, Peg disappeared up into the bus.

After a second, Laurel crawled aboard after her, trying to look suitably infirm and finding, after a touring in the Mexican sunshine, that it wasn't hard.

"What did I tell you!" Peg crowed triumphantly once the bus had started back up the hill with a jolting lunge. "This way we get back to the ship twenty minutes earlier and I can shed these shoes." She reached down to ease her heel from one of her pumps. "How did you like Elena?"

Laurel cast a wary glance around. "Should I be talking in my condition?"

"I think so—as long as you don't look too healthy."

"You don't have to worry about that. Elena

sounds like a handful. Casey could have problems before we get to Lima." Laurel leaned against the back of the seat and tried to relax. "Talk about a generation gap! I felt like Whistler's Mother when she sized me up."

"You can't be more than five years older than she is."

Laurel closed her eyes. "Age has nothing to do with it in Elena's case. I'm glad she's not my responsibility."

Peg made a noncommittal murmur.

"What does that mean?" Laurel asked, frowning slightly.

"When I was checking the cabin allotments last night, I noticed the Senorita Sanchez has been lodged in stateroom 112A."

"But that's right next to mine! Casey wouldn't pull such a sneaking trick. He simply couldn't."

Peg looked smug. "You don't think he's going to play nursemaid to Elena when Gwen Harper's standing in line for his free time."

Laurel grimaced with anger. "The man's a menace to everything in skirts. They should post stop signs around him like a dangerous intersection."

"Isn't it the truth! Groan a little, will you—the bus driver's watching and if you look like you're suffering, he'll drive faster."

They arrived back at the ship in good time without any additional dramatics on Laurel's part. After the rest of the tour group had gone back up the gangway, she assured the guide and the driver that she was feeling much better and thanked them for a pleasant day. They parted in an aura of international goodwill with enthusiastic handshakes all around.

When Laurel went aboard, she turned toward the stern stairs rather than heading for her stateroom. The promenade deck was blissfully deserted and she was able to lean on the rail and admire the activity on the dock below without having to make conversation.

By then, the cargo loading appeared completed and the drivers of the forklifts were heading their sturdy machines down the pier to a warehouse nearby. Two or three onlookers were still leaning against a flatbed rail car at the siding but the crowds that had greeted the *Traveler*'s arrival had disappeared. Laurel was willing to bet that the hot, humid air hanging over the port had much to do with the mass evacuation. Even in late afternoon there was scarcely a breeze stirring. The Gantry cranes at the ship's bow and stern were still, their gondola-like control cars already secured and deserted. The crew's leisure areas on deck were deserted, too—abandoned for the prospect of a few hours' leave ashore.

Music suddenly floated out from the main lounge amidships. Someone had activated the jukebox and the lilting refrain of "Tie a Yellow Ribbon on the Old Oak Tree" made Laurel tap her fingers on the rail.

Down on the dock, one of the loungers broke into an impromptu samba step and was applauded by his friends.

Laurel smiled and let her gaze move on up the road. She saw the usual group of uniformed officials bunched around the Mexican Customs office. As she watched, Casey came out of the office and paused in the doorway to shake hands all around before striding back down the deserted road toward the pier.

He had covered about half of the distance when Laurel saw a battered pickup truck come out from the side of a warehouse and accelerate as it hurtled down the middle of the road.

"Casey! Look out!" Laurel screamed at the top of her lungs.

There was no knowing whether it was her shout or the noise of the truck's engine that made Casey whirl and then dash for the curb in a burst of speed that would have done credit to a broken-field runner.

The truck swerved after him and, as Laurel screamed again, Casey dived head first over a boxwood hedge bordering the pavement. He lay sprawled atop it as the driver of the pickup yanked on his steering wheel to avoid the waist-high shrubbery. The tires squealed when the accelerator was floored once again and the truck shot between stacks of empty pallets on the dock and disappeared toward the other port gate a hundred feet beyond the *Traveler*'s bow.

As Laurel hung over the rail, she saw the vehicle swing onto the main highway without hesitating and merge in the traffic heading north.

She let out her breath in a rush, unaware till then that she'd been holding it. Her gaze darted back to Casey in the boxwood hedge. By then, he had slithered onto the ground and was standing shaking his left wrist which had evidently suffered in the plunge. As Laurel watched, his head came up slowly and his gaze met hers.

For an instant, he remained quiet. Then he retrieved his uniform cap from the dust, brushed it off, and put it back squarely on his head with a brevity of motion that indicated his temper was about to explode. As he marched painfully toward the ship, Laurel could see his lips moving. And as she hurried toward the gangway stairs to meet him, she was glad that Elena wasn't around—to add to her vocabulary.

Chapter Four

It took him longer to reach the foot of the gangway than she anticipated because the Customs officials in the hut finally rallied from their surprise and came hotfooting it down the street with a great thrashing of arms and indignant cries. The only thing they didn't do, Laurel thought irritably, was to send a volley of shots after the pickup. Since, by then, it had completely disappeared down the highway, even the officials recognized the futility of that gesture. But they were determined to wring the utmost from the situation.

Casey could be seen shaking his head violently when they urged him back to the Customs hut and the man who pulled out his notebook was given short shift as well. Everyone realized that the offender was long gone and while Casey could file a complaint, it would have little effect.

Casey verified it a few minutes later when he'd limped aboard and saw her waiting for him at the end of the gangway. "Got a minute?" he asked tersely.

"Of course ... but shouldn't you call Dr. Purcell?"

"There's nothing really hurt except my dignity—that's what I told those fellows." He jerked a head toward the Customs men who were walking back to their office. "Come on, you can get me a drink," he said, leading her down the deck to the purser's day room. Once inside, he made a disgusted gesture toward his uniform which bore graphic reminders of his plunge into the port shrubbery. "Lord, what a mess! It's a good thing I got rid of my moustache or I'd be combing boxwood out of it, as well." He tossed his cap toward the desk. "I think a shower is indicated even before the drink."

As Laurel bent over to pick up a twig which had fallen from his cuff, she searched for a lighthearted response and couldn't think of a thing. Now that some time had passed, her reaction to his mishap was making itself felt.

Casey paused halfway through his bedroom door to stare at her. "You look terrible . . . pale as one of Purcell's patients. What's the matter . . . was the tour too much for you?"

"No, of course not. I'm just not used to this heat." The lie came out quickly. "I'll be okay when the air-conditioning does its job."

"Ummm. I think you need restoring as much as I do. Better make that two drinks." His glance raked over her before he went on into the bedroom, shutting the door behind him.

A minute later, she heard the sound of the shower being turned on. She wandered restlessly over to the small bar in the corner, making Casey's drink and wondering whether to add gin to the tonic water in hers when the phone rang. Without thinking, she picked up the receiver.

"Is Casey around?" the chief officer asked hesitantly after she'd identified herself. "I need some information on the cargo figures."

"I'll see if I can find him," she replied diplomatically. "Hang on a minute." She laid the receiver on the desk top and then went back to put it in a desk drawer.

Fortunately, the sound of the shower had just stopped as she went over to the bedroom door and opened it a crack.

"Casey?"

"What is it?" He sounded almost as startled to hear her voice as the chief officer. "Wait a sec . . . I'm coming." The door was pulled all the way open before she could retreat and she heard his burst of laughter. "It's all right . . . you can open your eyes."

She signaled him to silence with an angry gesture. "Stop it, will you. The chief officer wants you on the phone."

"Okay." He pulled the belt of his terry-cloth robe tighter and tossed the towel he'd been using to dry his hair in the general direction of the bathroom. "Where in the devil did you hide the . . . oh, now I see it." Casey opened the drawer with an impatient yank and pulled out the receiver. "Yeah, Ted—what's the problem?"

Laurel found it difficult to keep her mind on the technical conversation that followed. It seemed as if the close brush with danger a little while before had sharpened her senses and powers of observation. Never before had she been so conscious of a man's physical presence. She was pulsatingly aware of Casey's lean strength as he stood by the desk . . . even of the way his terry-cloth robe strained at the shoulders when he reached for a clipboard hanging from a hook on the stateroom wall.

She dropped her glance and found herself staring at his muscular tanned legs in evidence below the knee-length robe, but when her eyes retreated upward, she was instantly aware of the thick dark hair on his chest as the robe parted. Feeling a surge of color blaze in her cheeks, she turned to stare out the porthole.

When Casey finally replaced the receiver she had herself under stern control. Fortunately, her reactions had gone unnoticed. Casey absently tightened the belt on his robe and moved away from the desk.

"Did you make that drink for me?" he asked.

Laurel half-turned and indicated it with her own glass.

"Thanks." He picked it up and took a deep swallow. "That tastes good. Why don't you sit down?" he asked, coming over beside her.

Laurie drew back hastily and then felt like a fool when she noticed his attention was on the pier below. She moved over to perch lightly on a chair arm. "Perhaps I should go. I imagine you want to get dressed."

"Not much point in it. I'll have to change for dinner in another fifteen minutes." He looked at her over his shoulder. "Unless this bothers you?" gesturing down at the robe.

"Heavens, no." She kept her voice as casual as his.

"I could lock the door but . . ."

"Don't you dare, then we *would* be in trouble. Maybe we are already—the chief officer sounded awfully suspicious."

"Ted? You're imagining things! Women have answered my telephone before."

"I'm sure of that." The remark came out before she could stop it.

Casey's features became impassive. "I was going to say that the stewardess used this typewriter for menus on the last trip. The keys were sticking on the chief steward's portable."

"Sorry—I owe you another apology."

"Don't bother. It was a normal reaction. To be honest, I'm beginning to think that you're the only normal woman on this cruise." He stared down at the ice in his drink. "That's why I wanted to ask you about the business down on the dock. You evidently saw the whole thing . . ."

She nodded reluctantly.

"I meant to thank you for shouting. It gave me some extra time for my swan dive into the shrubbery."

Laurel shuddered. "The front bumper of that truck was just inches behind you."

"I could feel it all the way," he said dryly. "Then there wasn't any doubt in your mind that he was trying to run me down?" As she looked up, puzzled, he added, "It could have been a drunk or a hot-head protesting American foreign policy."

Laurel thought about it for a moment and then shook her head emphatically. "Not a chance. I caught a glimpse of the driver's face—he was dead serious. Could it have been planned?"

"Anything's possible. There was a good chance I'd be down on the pier. A final check with the Customs people is part of my job."

"Didn't anybody recognize the truck?"

"They claimed they'd never seen it before."

Casey lit a cigarette and watched the smoke disintegrate. "Or, if they had, they weren't admitting it. We all agreed it must have been a drunk—it was the easy way out."

Laurie was watching him closely. "But you don't think so, do you?"

"It's a little too convenient." Casey picked up an ashtray from the desk and sat on the couch opposite her chair. "Maybe you've heard about some of the problems on this ship?" As she hesitated, he went on impatiently. "The U. S. Customs men practically took us apart looking for drugs when the *Traveler* docked in Long Beach after the last trip."

"You've been looking, too, haven't you?" Laurel was thinking out loud. "That's why you went back to sea again after a desk job."

He stubbed out his cigarette as if not wanting to bother with it any longer. "The main office thought maybe I could find out something. But I couldn't . . . not a damned thing. Neither could the Customs people—they even brought the Canine Corps in. The dogs sniffed their way through the crew's quarters and the passengers' staterooms and didn't find a thing."

"But why the *Traveler*? Why not some of the other Marden ships?"

"Because of our ports of call," he explained. "On the homeward route, we usually stop at Colombia just before the U. S. The narcotics people know that one of the main arteries of drug traffic runs through there before heading north. Overland, it funnels through Mexico. If the smugglers can get the contraband aboard ship, it cuts travel time getting it to market."

Laurel took a sip of her drink and then put it on the table at her side. "How do they find out about the shipments in the first place?"

"Informants. And the latest word is that something big is brewing."

"Who do you suspect?"

He grimaced and shook his head. "Even the crew has been picked clean for this trip. We were taking no chances." His slow grin broke through. "That's one reason for the inexperienced waiters and stewards."

She put up a solemn hand. "I'll stop complaining about the dining room service as of now."

"Well, at least it explains the cold water in the finger bowls."

Her eyes widened. "Who has finger bowls? I thought it was great when I had a saucer under my coffee cup for breakfast."

Casey winced visibly. "Don't let the chief steward hear you or he'll have your waiter keelhauled. For the prices Marden charges, the passengers expect finger bowls." Then he shook his head as if to clear it. "How in the devil did we get sidetracked to that?"

"Search me." She was amused at his annoyance. "I take it the officers have been cleared of suspicion, too."

"Of course. What brought that to your mind?"

"Well, Dr. Purcell mentioned this was his last trip. He didn't sound happy about it." She essayed the information tentatively.

Casey frowned down at his drink. "Oh, George. It's a damned shame . . . but he drinks too much. On the last few trips, it's interfered with his work and we can't allow that. It was too bad that he had trouble the night we left the States."

She brushed that aside. "Casey . . . the man who tried to run you down. Has anything like that ever happened before?"

He shook his head. "That's why I wanted your opinion. I thought I was imagining things. Maybe we both are. But if we're not . . ."

"Then you're getting closer to the truth than you thought." She bit her lip. "There are other kinds of contraband from this part of the world, aren't there? Besides drugs, I mean?"

"Sure. The usual—objets d'art, jewels, gold—take your choice. At one time, Inca treasure was big."

"So we don't know exactly what we're looking for, either."

"Well, we can eliminate the white slave trade. Container cargo discourages that." He stood up then and moved over to the bar. "Can I freshen your drink?"

"No, thanks." She broke off as a knock sounded and the office door was abruptly pushed open. Gwen Harper stood poised in the doorway.

"Casey, honey . . ." The actress stopped in the middle of her effusive greeting when she saw Laurel. Amazement, then frowning suspicion washed over her face as she surveyed them. "I didn't know you were entertaining. And so informally, too," she added, noting his robe.

If Casey was discomfited, it didn't show. "Informal parties are the best kind. Sit down and join us, Gwen. Can I get you a drink?"

His cool response spiked her guns. "No . . . not now, thanks."

"Well, at least come in and close the door."

Automatically she did as he asked and then stood by it. "Actually I wanted you to call the carpenter," she murmured.

"Chips? He'll be back on duty as soon as we sail. That shouldn't be long. What's the trouble?"

"One of my bureau drawers is stuck." Gwen's defensive manner showed she was searching for a plausible excuse.

The thought evidently had occurred to Casey because he said laconically, "My lord, half the bureau drawers on this ship are stuck . . . including mine." Then, at her suddenly stormy expression, he relented. "I know that's no excuse. I'll send Chips around."

"I felt you'd take care of it, sweetie." Gwen's smile was triumphant when she turned to Laurel. "Casey's absolutely marvelous at details and I did want everything shipshape at my cocktail party tonight. Perhaps you'd like to join us," she added as if she'd just thought of it. "There'll be the captain and the Countess, of course . . ." She ticked them off on manicured fingers. "Eduardo's bringing Elena . . . I don't think you've met her."

"Yes, she did. At the hotel in Manzanillo," Casey put in.

"That's better still. The chief officer said he'd try to look in and, of course, Casey . . ."

"It's kind of you," Laurel's voice was only faintly polite, "but I'm afraid I've made other plans."

Gwen's expression showed she didn't believe it. "Are you sure? We'd love to have you—wouldn't we, Casey?"

Before he could reply, Laurel stood up and replaced her glass on the bar. "I'm sorry. Perhaps some other time. Now, if you'll excuse me . . ."

"Oh, no!" Gwen protested prettily. "I didn't mean to interrupt *anything*. Now that I've accomplished what I've come for . . ." She opened the door and smiled at both of them. "I'll see you later."

Laurel watched her leave and then shot an angry glance at Casey.

He shrugged. "Sorry about that. Gwen's inclined to chew the scenery wherever she is. It's a way of life with actresses. Why don't you come along to the party?"

"No, thanks." Laurel moved over to the door and stood with her hand on the knob. "If there's nothing else . . ."

He was watching her steadily. "Not really. Thanks for coming along. I hope you weren't embarrassed by Gwen's interruption. Maybe I should have gotten dressed, after all."

Her expression froze. "Don't be silly. There was certainly no reason to feel guilty."

"Well, don't worry about it. I'll make sure that Gwen keeps quiet. If you change your mind about the party, come on along."

"No . . . I really do have other plans."

His gaze held hers mockingly. "Besides, you never stand in line. I should think that would limit your social calendar."

"It hasn't been a burden so far. Thank you for the drink."

He sobered instantly, aware that he'd pushed his teasing too far. "The thanks should be on my side. After this afternoon, I'm in your debt. If you hadn't shouted at the crucial moment, I'd be nursing a hell of a lot more than a pulled muscle now." He ran a finger gently down her flushed cheek. "Thanks, honey."

Casey's generous apology stayed with Laurel and softened her mood for the rest of the evening. It even allowed her to greet Eduardo's late arrival at dinner with a smile and to return Gwen's wave when she made her dramatic walk to the captain's table. Behind her, Elena Sanchez, who had changed to a brightly flowered dress, was quietly seated at Casey's table.

"The chief steward squeezed in another place," Eduardo remarked, following her glance. "Elena wouldn't have it any other way." He handed Laurel a menu. "Why didn't you come to the party? Gwen said she'd asked you."

Laurel was tempted to say that an invitation didn't constitute a royal command but when she saw the Purcells coming to join them, she simply murmured, "I had other things to do," and changed the subject. After that, dinner proceeded slowly, but the food and conversation were good enough that no one really minded Rip's serving mishaps. The only disconcerting thing about the meal for Laurel was encountering Casey's gaze when she happened to look toward his table. The first time, she felt it was coincidence, but when it occurred again, she wondered uncomfortably what was behind his brooding mien.

When dinner was over, she didn't linger to find out. After exchanging a few words with Gwen in the lounge foyer, she excused herself to Eduardo.

"Don't tell me you're going to disappear again," he complained. "I haven't seen you all day. If you don't want to sit through the miserable movie tonight, we can relax on the deck with an after-dinner drink. It's a beautiful night and there's hardly a ripple on the water. Besides, if you leave me alone, I'll have Elena on my hands again. *Dios!* I'm old enough to be her father."

Laurie grinned at him. "I'll bet it's the first time Elena Sanchez has raised paternal feelings in any man."

"Right now, I'm struggling with another kind of feeling, *Laurita mia,*" he warned her softly.

"Then it's just as well I'm going below." From the corner of her eye, she could see Casey coming through the lounge and she wasn't disposed to linger. "See you tomorrow, Eduardo. Give Elena my best."

Three hours later, the Mexican girl knocked on Laurie's cabin door to return the greeting in person.

"I hoped you'd still be up," she said as Laurel appeared in a lounging robe. "Could I come in for a few minutes?"

"Of course. I wasn't asleep," Laurel said truthfully, trying not to stare at the shortie gown and robe that Elena was wearing in the public corridor. The white cotton outfit trimmed with a gay rickrack braid made the girl look young and appealing. Unfortunately, the bright hall lights also revealed the transparency of the material and Laurel hastily ushered her in before she shocked a stray passerby.

"Sit over there on the chair," she said, following Elena into the cabin. "It's fairly comfortable. I'll sit on the bed."

Elena watched her go over and pull the rumpled bed-covering to a semblance of order.

"You *were* in bed," she accused. "Casey was right—he said not to bother you."

"Casey was talking through his hat. He doesn't know anything about my personal habits," Laurel said.

Elena interpreted that literally. "He wasn't wearing a hat. It was when we were in the lounge after the movie. I think it was the movie that gave me the pain."

Laurel paused in her bedmaking, "What are you talking about?"

"The pain in my head. Here." Elena clutched her forehead like the victim in a television commercial. "I tried to go to sleep but that only made it worse. Now I have the neck ache, too."

"Maybe you should see Dr. Purcell."

"*Dios,* no. All I need is some aspirin . . . I forgot to pack any."

"Well, if you're sure aspirin will do the trick," Laurel stood up and rummaged in the bureau drawer. "Would Casey approve of your taking this?"

Elena made herself more comfortable in the armchair. "I didn't mention the headache to Casey . . . he acts enough like my papa as it is."

Laurie stifled a grin as she handed over the small bottle. Poor Elena was having a hard time of it if both Eduardo and Casey insisted on treating her like the schoolgirl she was. "Take it along. I have another one in my purse." As Laurel went back to sit on the bed, she added diplomatically, "I'm sure Mr. Waring doesn't treat you differently from the rest of the women on the ship."

"Hah!" Elena sounded disgusted. "You should

have seen the way he flirted with that actress . . . Senora Harper."

"I didn't know she was married."

"She's not—now," Elena cut in ruthlessly. "I heard her telling the Countess at the cocktail party. Casey made me drink orange juice all the time I was there." Her features pulled down in a scowl. "Even tonight, after the movie I had to drink more juice."

"It's very good for you," Laurel said, trying to be tactful.

"Then why do I have the headache?"

"I'm not sure." Laurel brushed her hair back from her hot cheek. "I have one, too—and I didn't drink any orange juice."

"I . . . I didn't know." Elena's features sobered. "I'm sorry—did you want to be alone?"

"Of course not," Laurel smiled. "It's not a bad headache. And I'm happy to have some company."

"*Bueno*. So am I." Once Elena dropped her attempt at surface sophistication, she was easy to like. "Tomorrow I'm to help you wrap Christmas presents for the passengers—Casey promised I could. Gwen wanted to help, too, but Casey said she was doing enough by reading the Nativity story at the Christmas Eve service. He seemed pretty damned surprised when she said you'd asked her after dinner."

"You shouldn't swear," Laurie murmured automatically, before adding, "Why should he be surprised? After all, she *is* an actress. I thought he'd be pleased."

Elena's shrug was so Latin that she might have been a carbon copy of Eduardo.

"If he doesn't approve," Laurel went on crossly, "he can do his own arranging after this."

"He didn't say anything," Elena replied, striving to make things clear, "but he didn't look happy. Especially when Gwen announced it at the midnight buffet."

Laurel glanced automatically at her watch. It was just past ten; Casey was even right about the timing of the buffet.

"He said that Mrs. Purcell needed more time for her craft class or she would do it," Elena reported.

"Do what?" Laurel wasn't concentrating enough on the other's conversation.

"Wrap presents with us tomorrow. I *told* you."

"So you did." Laurel poked her pillow behind her and tried to find a comfortable position that didn't involve putting her head in the lampshade of her reading light. "What's the matter with Peg's craft class?"

"That's what Casey asked," Elena confided. "Mrs. Purcell said the women didn't like eyeglass cases so she's promised them something extra exciting tomorrow and it's going to take more time."

"I see."

"Casey didn't," Elena said. "He didn't think a craft class project needed to be thrilling, but the captain said it was about time something was a surprise on this trip. He said things were so dull that if they scraped the hull they'd find ivy instead of barnacles."

"Oh, ho! I'll bet the Countess liked that!" Laurel murmured, grinning despite herself. "What happened next at the party?" Laurel knew that she shouldn't have encouraged Elena, but her narrative was too fascinating to stop.

The younger girl shrugged. "Not much more. About that time the waiter who works at your table in the dining room . . ."

"You mean Rip?"

Elena nodded vigorously. *"Sí,* that was his name . . . well, he tripped and spilled the tureen of shrimp dip down the front of Gwen's dress. *Aye de mi!* You should have heard her! What words that woman knows! Long ones and short ones!" Elena's look of admiration changed to sadness. "That's when Eduardo took me away. Gwen had to change her dress before dinner."

"That makes sense. Shrimp dip doesn't do much for decoration."

"Not on white chiffon with a neckline down to here." Elena pointed to the neighborhood of her navel. *"Verdad?"*

The two of them stared at each other for a long moment and then burst out laughing.

"I should be ashamed of myself," Laurel said finally, "but for some reason my headache feels much better."

Elena got to her feet, pulling her robe together with one hand and clutching the bottle of aspirin with the other. "So does mine. My neck's still stiff, though."

Laurel followed her to the stateroom door. "I know a better remedy for that than aspirin. May I show you?"

"Pero sí," Elena looked mystified but led the way into her stateroom which was almost a twin of Laurel's. "Now what is this *remedio* for a pain in the neck?"

Laurel marched over to the bed and grasped a pillow stuffed like a hard sausage. "You could have called your steward but we'd be back in Long Beach before he appeared," she said, starting to peel off pillowcases.

Elena's eyes were wide as she saw the fifth pillowcase hit the floor. "I don't understand ... is it an American custom?"

"Only for people who like a pain in the neck," Laurel said after she'd reached the blue ticking plus one. She gathered the extra linen and dumped it in the laundry hamper in Elena's bathroom. "There! Everything should be all right now. Better get some sleep. I need a good helper in the morning wrapping those presents." She smiled over her shoulder as she headed for the door, "I never could tie bows."

"*Momento* ... Laurel. May I call you Laurel?" Elena asked her.

"Of course."

"Thank you for being so nice to me. Casey said you were ... okay."

Laurel's smile widened. "So are you. G'night, Elena. Sleep well."

When Laurel reported to the chief purser's office the next day she found Elena waiting with a towering stack of presents on the couch. Wrapping paper and ribbon were piled neatly on the chair beside her. They worked until the deck lunch and afterwards through most of the afternoon before they finally finished.

When the last bow was tied, Elena disappeared for a shuffleboard date she'd persuaded Eduardo to make during lunch. Laurel declined an invitation to keep score for them and strolled out by the pool to get some fresh air. Not surprisingly, she saw the tanned form of the chief purser in swim trunks stretched on a lounge nearby.

As she approached, he warily opened an eye and then closed it again. Laurel moved over to him, keeping her glance averted from his expanse of tanned chest. "I hope I'm not disturbing you," she lied, deliberately blotting out the sun. "You must be exhausted . . . avoiding work all day. How do you manage it?"

Casey opened his eyes and pushed up on one elbow when he realized she wasn't going to leave him in peace. "It's a terrible job. Are the presents wrapped?"

"Naturally." Laurel decided it would be nice if he offered her an empty neighboring lounge and her lips thinned when she saw he had no intention of it. "Plus the other 'suggestions' you mentioned in your note."

Her tone of voice made him eye her thoughtfully. "I did hang around waiting for you a while after breakfast. Then I had other things to do. I thought that waiter of yours had improved."

"He did," she snapped. "This morning, circumstances were beyond his control."

"I don't get it."

She sighed. "Rip didn't either. That was the whole trouble." At Casey's sudden frown she went on to explain, "Elena has a new T-shirt that she wore to breakfast. Unfortunately, she walked through the dining room with her arms crossed over her chest."

"So?"

"All we could see were the words 'Sex is a . . .' Rip dropped the coffee pot when he tilted his head trying to read the rest of the slogan. It took fifteen minutes to clean up the mess."

Casey shook his head sorrowfully. "The boy goes from one catastrophe to another."

"It really wasn't his fault this morning," Laurel pointed out. "Every man in the dining room was doing the same thing."

"Then for the sake of the carpet, I'm glad they weren't all pouring coffee. I'll tell Elena to stow that outfit." He cocked an eyebrow at her. "Unless you could manage to."

"Oh, no! Ask Peg Purcell to play mother if you feel it's necessary. Although," she added thoughtfully, "I haven't seen her all day."

"Then you didn't try the Inca Lounge. The craft class has gone on to bigger and better things. Half the women on the ship were up there working on outfits for the costume party and talent show. Peg had the chief steward buy beads and junk jewelry in Manzanillo. There's enough glitter for a Las Vegas chorus line."

Laurie started to smile. "But there the similarity stops."

"Right. But if the passengers want jeweled belts . . ." Casey shrugged. "It's a small price to pay." He leaned back and closed his eyes again.

It was an obvious dismissal, but Laurel lingered, determined to irritate him. "I'm glad to see that you can relax," she said in a tone that meant nothing of the sort. "I thought a chief purser's job kept him busy all the time. Of course, I didn't realize he had to bother with things like stuck drawers. How *is* Miss Harper, by the way?"

His eyes opened just a slit. "In better shape than her drawers, thanks. I'll tell her you asked."

She subdued an urge to throttle him. "Do that. You're sure you don't have any other jobs you want done?"

He shook his head. "It's this way," he drawled. "By rights, I should be busier than a mosquito on a bikini beach, but I've found from experience that it's best to do one thing at a time."

"Oh?"

"Uh-huh." He shifted his hips on the lounge to take advantage of the sun. "Right now I'm going to take my nap and get that over with. See you, sweetie."

After that Laurel was glad when the captain asked her to award prizes for the bingo game after dinner. With a casual disregard for the purser's budget, she distributed goodies with a lavish hand. When she finished, all the passengers were beaming and Casey was regarding her as if he'd found a viper coiled under his lifeboat cover.

"Those prizes were supposed to last until Lima. Now I'll have to replenish our stock in San Salvador," he hissed as he passed her on the dance floor.

"I just followed the rules," she said, wide-eyed. "The captain said, 'Give away prizes,' so I did."

"All you could find in the damned closet?"

"Exactly." Then as Eduardo pulled her away, she said over her shoulder in deliberate mimicry, "See you, sweetie." As an exit line, she thought it was even better the second time around.

The next day, she decided to call a truce in view of the holiday season. She met Casey for the first time beside the Christmas tree he was having erected in the main lounge.

"Anything I can do to help?" Laurel asked when he was alone for a moment.

He glanced at her sternly, his stubborn jaw much in evidence above his crisp white uniform shirt. The afternoon by the pool had deepened his tan and banished the fatigue lines around his eyes. This morning he looked like a man capable of dealing with anything—even recalcitrant secretaries. "I don't know why it is," he said conversationally, "but every time I'm with you, I feel as if a fuse is sizzling and something's about to blow. Usually it's the top of my head."

She surveyed him just as solemnly. "Possibly in honor of the holiday, we might declare a truce. Besides, who could fight in here?" She gestured to include the lounge which was crowded with passengers doing their best to transform it into the Christmas scene. Some men were busily laying out the strings of lights destined for the plump fir tree, others were arranging colored spotlights overhead. The uncombed Miss Scott had a group of women looping red and green crepe paper around every pillar in sight while Eduardo inspected tree ornaments. Even Gwen Harper was instructing a waiter on the proper way to hang wreaths in the long windows.

Elena, in a demure blouse and skirt, was at the electric organ diligently practicing carols. Casey must have delivered his warning on her costume, Laurel decided. It was a good thing, because the retired Baptist minister was holding a songbook for her.

"This place looks like Tom Sawyer's fence," Laurel said admiringly, as she turned back to Casey. "What else is on the schedule?"

"Complimentary champagne at the cocktail hour with S. Claus distributing the presents."

"You can't have the real St. Nick stored in your closet—I would have found him when I was digging out the prizes last night."

"Don't I know it," he said ruefully. "The chief officer is the only one aboard whose waistline fits our costume. After dinner, it's community singing and a film short on 'Christmas Around the World' before the midnight service." Seeing her eyebrows climb, he added irritably, "You needn't look like that! The film's okay ... pretty damn good as a matter of fact."

She grinned at him. "Stop being so sensitive. It sounds fabulous. Christmas at home was never like this."

"It was better for a lot of these people," Casey told her, shoving his hands in his pockets. "That's why we keep them so busy that they don't have time to think about it. Like Eduardo."

"You're right. I'd forgotten for a minute."

"Well, make sure you remember it when you get back to your desk in the advertising department." He stood up and added briskly, "You can help put the ornaments on after they string the lights, then bring in those presents you wrapped. We'll put them around the base of the tree."

The rest of the day worked as smoothly as Casey's schedule. The passengers seemed to realize that their holiday depended on their enthusiasm and turned to work with a will. Judging by appearances, the crew was imbued with the same spirit. It was evident in the men's faces and their obvious pride in the beautifully decorated ship.

Later on, the Christmas Eve dinner was an occa-

sion to be remembered, from the magnificent food to the holly-red bow ties worn by the waiters.

Champagne was still flowing at dessert time but Laurel's peace of mind vanished abruptly when she saw Gwen being discreetly supported by the captain and the Countess as they left the table.

Unless the actress sobered up considerably before the midnight service, she'd never find the lectern—let alone the Bible.

"What's wrong, *querida*?" Eduardo murmured as they prepared to follow the Purcells from the dining room. "You look as if you suddenly had a pain."

"No, I'm fine," she said, trying to smile as she wondered what to do. She could scarcely ask Eduardo to sober up the redhead. On the other hand . . . she *could* ask Casey.

But when they got to the lounge, the chief purser's dress uniform was not in evidence. His assistant was the one who led the community singing. Laurel watched in misery as Gwen Harper concentrated on a steady stream of champagne cocktails throughout the program.

By the time the movie was over, Laurel was seriously contemplating luring Gwen into a storeroom and locking the door behind her. It wouldn't be easy because the actress was then sitting on a bar stool drinking with the chief engineer. The only way to make her move, Laurel thought dismally, would be to sound the emergency alarm. Her gaze went over to the captain who was deep in conversation with the Countess. He didn't look like a man who would choose that moment for a lifeboat drill.

At fifteen minutes before midnight, Laurel was

approaching sheer hysteria. She hurried up the stairs to the Inca Lounge just minutes ahead of the serpentine of passengers destined for the same place. By then, she was ready to Indian wrestle Gwen to keep her away from the pulpit if necessary.

At that moment, Laurel saw Casey come in the other door of the lounge to make a last-minute check of the room.

Desperately she brushed past the table by the door with programs and Bibles stacked upon it and sidled through the rows of chairs. "Casey . . . thank God! Where have you been?" Without giving him a chance to answer, she said, "It's Gwen—she's absolutely reeling. What are we going to do?"

He bent to rearrange a chair. "There's no need to worry . . . it's all taken care of."

"What do you mean 'taken care of'? She'll be here in five minutes . . ." Hastily she lowered her voice as the passengers started surging into the lounge. "You'll have to take her to your cabin," she continued in an urgent whisper.

"No way! My 'goodwill for the holidays' doesn't go that far. Besides, she's not even coming up here. I told her earlier that we'd offend the judge if we didn't let him read the Christmas story. He does it every year at his home church." Casey pulled Laurel toward the rear of the lounge as the last chairs filled and a uniformed crewman sat down at the piano to open his music. "Relax. Let's enjoy this."

Despite the strange surroundings, or perhaps because of them, the traditional carol service had seldom seemed more beautiful. If the choir lacked technical merit, it was overflowing in enthusiasm, and the elderly voice of the judge quietly recounting the Christmas story was exactly right. By the time Captain Samuels, impressive in his white dress uniform, read the benediction, there was scarcely a dry eye in the place.

Laurel automatically accepted Casey's handkerchief and blew her nose while the pianist thundered out "It Came Upon the Midnight Clear" for the recessional.

"Stick around," Casey murmured when she would have followed the last row of passengers. "We have to stack the hymnals afterwards."

"Oh, of course." She bent meekly to pick up the books and told herself fiercely that she should remember Casey didn't let any woman interfere with his job—he'd made that abundantly clear. She watched him go over to the young pianist and thank him for the accompaniment. There was some good-natured banter between them before the man collected his music, closed the keyboard, and disappeared down the inside stairs.

The sudden quiet that descended in the room made Laurel grope for something to break it. "It was a beautiful service," she said, taking the last load of hymnals over to the door as Casey pushed the lectern back against the wall. "I didn't know it would be so impressive. Somehow being out at sea . . . and so isolated . . ." She bent her head as she stacked the books. "It's hard to explain," she finished shyly, "but I'll never forget it."

There was a silence and she looked up to find Casey staring at her. Their glance held for a moment or two—then he swept some papers from the top of the lectern and went over to open the door leading onto the afterdeck. "Leave that," he told her. "The stewards will take care of it when they clear. Let's get some air."

Silently she did as he asked. By mutual inclination, they turned to the short flight of stairs leading up to the glassed-observation bridge. Laurel gathered her long skirt when it would have whipped in the wind before they reached the platform.

"Seems strange that we're the only ones up here again," she said as they pulled to a stop and leaned against the padded bench. "It's such a lovely night."

"It's been a long day and there's a busier one tomorrow. Probably we're the ones who need our heads examined," Casey remarked, but she noticed that even as he said it, he took a deep breath of fresh air and settled more comfortably against the bench beside her.

Her eyes widened as a sudden thought struck her. "Casey—if we're in port tomorrow—there could be more trouble for you."

"You mean a repeat version in Acajutla of the attempt at Manzanillo?" His grin was a white slash across his shadowed face. "They'd have a hell of a time—the dock is too narrow. One of us would end up in the briny."

"You know what I mean."

"Sure, but there's no use fussing. Believe me, I'll be looking over my shoulder all the time. Probably I made too much of the other. Most likely, it was some laborer who wanted to see me take a header in the shrubbery. He probably got a big laugh at the *cantina* that night."

"Umm. Maybe." It was plain he hadn't convinced her.

"Anyhow, it's not the thing to think about on a holiday."

She smiled in sudden delight. "This *is* Christmas, isn't it? I'm still not convinced it's real."

"You'd better believe it." He checked his watch by the pale gleam of moonlight. "We're well into the festive day and morning will be here before we know it. Are you going to San Salvador with the shore party?"

Laurel nodded. "Yes, of course. Shall I count noses like before?"

"Not this time. I'm tagging along, too. Have to see a man about some prizes when we get into town," he added wryly. "If he'll even answer the phone on Christmas."

A dimple flickered by the corner of her mouth. "Sorry about that . . ."

"The devil you are. You enjoyed every minute of it," he grinned. "It's just a good thing I didn't store your Christmas present in the closet along with the rest of the loot."

"My present!" She stared up at his face, forgetting for the moment about the deck beneath their feet and their isolated aerie under the stars. Even the gentle motion of the bow cutting through the swells was hardly discernible and the faint refrain of "Jingle Bells" floating upward through the night air from the jukebox two decks below scarcely registered. "You shouldn't have bothered," she protested feebly as he pulled a small package from his inside jacket pocket and gave it to her.

"Go ahead . . . open it," he instructed. "After all, it's Christmas."

His command was all Laurel needed. She tore off the bright wrapping and opened a leather case to find a silver pin shaped like a tiny bird cage complete with an exquisite turquoise bird on a perch.

"It's perfectly beautiful," she murmured in awed tones. "Thank you so much!"

Casey's slight smile showed that he was pleased by her response and he watched as she pinned the brooch carefully on her silk mandarin blouse.

"There!" She tucked in her chin to admire it when she'd finished. "The color of the bird is just perfect for this outfit," she added, smoothing her skirt with its variegated shades of blue and green. Then her pleased expression faded. "But I feel terrible . . . I don't have a present for you."

"Certainly you have, Laurie." His tone was soft . . . suggestive. "You don't even have to wrap it up," he added as she started to protest. "I'll take delivery right now."

Laurie knew an instant's panic as she saw his head come down and his lips covered hers. The kiss began as a gentle quest but as Casey felt her involuntary response, his mouth hardened, forcing her to obey his will. She trembled as she felt his hands explore her back before they moved purposefully down to pull her even closer.

Laurel felt as if she were drowning in the sweetness of the embrace when Casey finally raised his lips just far enough to mutter, "I've wanted to do this since the first night you came on board." Then before she could attempt an answer, his mouth came down again in a kiss that was even more assured and devastating than the first.

Laurel finally pushed away—almost with desperation. "Casey—that's enough!" She was breathing hard as she attempted to rearrange her blouse and regain a modicum of sanity. "More than enough," she murmured shakily.

Casey straightened and stared down at her with an enigmatic expression. Then, he shrugged and leaned against the end of the bench. "I enjoyed it. If you're honest, you'll admit it was long overdue."

She took a deep breath as she tried to think. Honesty wasn't necessarily the best policy when a man held beliefs like Casey's. He wasn't proclaiming any undying love, she noticed. His satisfaction was strictly concerned with physical pleasure.

"I thought," she said, stalling for time, "we were simply exchanging greetings of the season." Her tone was so light and uncaring that she congratulated herself and went on. "Besides, I don't hold philosophical discussions in the moonlight."

Casey's eyebrows climbed. "So be it! Is it okay if I say I liked your present?"

She nodded, keeping her glance averted. "I liked yours, too. So we're even."

"Not quite." He was still watching her closely. "There's Boxing Day tomorrow and a whole fistful of saints' days before New Year's. This is just the beginning of present-giving."

"I wouldn't count on it," she flashed back, nursing her pride. "This interlude hasn't changed a thing . . . for either of us."

"Hasn't it?" His tone was level. "Why don't you

agree that we've been attracted to each other from the beginning? It's a normal enough reaction."

Laurel could have told him that just then she was feeling far from normal, but she had no intention of it. Apparently his pulse had settled back to a steady beat while hers was still leaping out of control. "I'm not worried about my libido," she told him. "And I'd rather not get in a pointless argument at this time of night discussing clinical reactions. I think we'd better go. Thank you again for my present."

He inclined his head gravely. "Thank you for mine. Merry Christmas, Laurie. Sleep well," he urged softly, "and pleasant dreams."

"Merry Christmas, Casey." The words came out with difficulty because suddenly she wanted to cry. As she left him and fled down the stairs, she knew that any chance of sleeping well for the rest of the night was going to be impossible. And as for the dreams—they didn't even bear thinking about.

Chapter Five

Christmas morning arrived bathed in gentle sunshine.

The balmy weather was hard to reconcile with the date on the calendar, but as Laurel stared down at the narrow dock in Acajutla, the main port for El Salvador, she decided the unseasonable novelty was delightful.

It was difficult to brush aside the rest of her feelings. Normally she wouldn't have chosen to spend Christmas at a Central American pier stacked high with bags of coffee and baled cotton. Then she saw the banner stretched between pillars that read *Bienvenido amigos—Feliz Navidad,* and began to realize that some places didn't need tinsel and colored lights to celebrate the festive day. Acajutla had the proper feeling if not the trappings.

As Laurel's gaze went forward to the bow of the ship, she saw a sturdy fir tree had been proudly attached to the uppermost crossbar of the forward mast. Below it, strings of colored lights wound downward, ready for nighttime display. The *Traveler* was all dressed up in her holiday finery, too, and suddenly seemed like home.

Laurel brushed her wet lashes impatiently.

This was no time to be acting like a sentimental idiot. Probably she was feeling more vulnerable than usual after a night spent tossing in her stateroom bed.

The interlude with Casey on the flying bridge had been a mistake. The only thing it had proved to Laurel was what she'd suspected all along: that there was no way for her to win in a contest with him. She'd emerged from it more miserable than ever because now she had to admit her strong physical attraction where before there'd been a reasonable doubt.

She studiously avoided the word "love" because she knew that the term didn't exist in the chief purser's vocabulary. In his ground rules for the female sex, Casey's aims weren't complicated. At midnight on a moonlit deck, he could rely on technique and let body chemistry do the rest.

Laurel's lips quirked as she thought about it. If Casey needed any testimonials, she could certainly furnish them. He'd never know how hard it was for her to leave his embrace and go down to her stateroom alone. Only the thought of being another willing victim to his practiced charm strengthened her resistance. But it didn't help her to sleep. Or keep her from wondering for the next five hours if she'd made the right decision. And now that another day had dawned, she knew that she'd have to keep right on fighting her inclinations. Casey's chemistry may have required moonlight and music but Laurel had made the appalling discovery that she didn't need any of the romantic background. She wanted him just as much in the cold light of dawn.

All of which was enough to give her a decided

headache. She rubbed her hand wearily against her forehead and decided to go find an aspirin.

"*Laurita,* I've been looking all over for you." Eduardo showed up beside her, immaculate as usual in a lightweight blazer and slacks. "Are you going on that accursed group tour?" He jerked his head toward the pier where a bus was being carefully directed to the gangway.

She shaded her eyes as she glanced up at him. "Why, yes. I thought everybody was."

"I could have hired a car if I'd found you earlier," he grumbled. "Where have you been hiding?"

"I had coffee in my room . . . I wasn't hungry," she evaded.

"No matter. At least we can be together on the bus today. I hope you're making Casey do some work for a change."

"He said that he'd be along. Today I'm just a passenger." Although she spoke calmly, her thoughts were racing on ahead. The only sensible thing for her to do was to accept Eduardo's bid as an escort. No harm could come to either of them and he'd be a willing buffer in her dealings with Casey.

"Then you'd better get your hat. The bus is leaving in ten minutes." He was watching her closely. "Do you feel all right? You look tired."

"I'm a little short on sleep, but I'll be fine. Shall I meet you on the bus?"

"If you like, I'll go along and get our seats." He walked beside her to open the door to the lounge. "Take your time—I won't let them leave without you. After all, it's a holiday." His expression was gentle as he added, "Happy Christmas, Laurel. I'm glad I found you under my tree this year."

His words made her pause. Then she impulsively stood on tiptoe to kiss his cheek. "Thanks, Eduardo. That's the nicest present yet." She reached for his hand. "Friends?"

"Friends—definitely." He smiled back at her and brought her fingertips up to his lips for a gentle caress.

The sound of a door closing at the other end of the room made them glance over their shoulders to see Casey's uniformed figure disappearing out on deck.

Laurel felt a twinge of dismay that Casey had seen the affectionate byplay but she relaxed as she followed Eduardo to the stairs. Perhaps it was the best thing that could have happened. At least she had served notice to Mr. Waring that she wasn't lacking for masculine companionship.

It was evident that Casey wasn't suffering a dearth of female company either when she encountered him later at the bus with Gwen on one side and Elena, looking rebellious, on the other.

"I don't see why you can't sit with me," the younger girl was complaining to him as she started up the steps.

"Because, *chica*, I've made other arrangements. Here's Miss Cavanaugh, she'll take over," he added.

Laurel felt his usual top-to-toe appraisal. Probably he was noting the smudges of weariness under her eyes and filing the information away for later, she thought angrily before she asked, "Take over what?"

"Me," Elena said, pausing halfway. "Casey,

thinks I should go sit by myself and look at the damned scenery——"

"Watch your language," Casey cut in.

Laurel heard herself saying, "Come sit with me, Elena," and wished for the second time that morning that she didn't work for the steamship company, too. It would have made mutiny a lot easier. "Eduardo's saving some places on the bus."

"He wants to be with you—he won't want me along."

Laurel smiled reassuringly at the young, doleful face. "Of course he will."

Casey looked annoyed. "For God's sake, this is just a bus tour. There's nothing to get icky-sticky about."

"Then why are you getting so mad?" Elena asked. "And what's 'icky-sticky'?"

Laurel stepped into the breach before he could answer. "We're holding up traffic, honey," she said to Elena and urged her gently up the steps.

Eduardo beckoned from the back of the bus. When he saw Elena was in the party, he merely said, "If we move to the back seat, there'll be room for all of us."

Surprisingly, Gwen had followed them down the aisle and sat in the double seat that Eduardo vacated. Shortly afterwards, she was joined by Peg Purcell who waved cheerfully at Laurel and mouthed "See you later," before sitting down on the aisle seat.

The bus pulled out right after that with Laurel wondering why Casey hadn't boarded; she was certain that he'd be with Gwen.

Elena solved the mystery as she peered down from her window and announced, "Casey's car has passed us already . . . the driver went ahead as soon as we got off the pier."

Peg turned to say over her shoulder, "Don't worry, Elena, he'll wait for us at the first stop. We're all going to the same places today."

"I'd still rather be in his car," Elena announced to the world at large.

"If you keep that up, I'll have the driver drag you on a rope behind the bus," Eduardo told her firmly. "Casey invited the judge and his wife to ride with him so they'd be more comfortable. Tour buses are hard on old bones. And middle-aged ones, too," he added as the driver went up the dirt road from the harbor without slackening speed.

"I'm too excited to think about such things," Laurel confessed. "This is the first time I've ever been to El Salvador. To be honest, I wasn't even sure where to look for it in the atlas. And don't tell me the natives haven't missed me," she warned as he started to laugh.

"I wouldn't think of it," he assured her. "You aren't the first tourist to arrive like that, but you'll probably come back again. Most people do. There is the scenery—" he pointed to the lush green fields on either side of the bus—"and, of course, the volcanoes." His gesture encompassed the rugged mountain chain in the distance with distinctive cone-shaped tops on several of the peaks. "There are one hundred eighty-seven in all—with twenty-two active ones. Volcanoes are a mixed blessing for the people here."

She turned to look at him. "Why is that?"

"Well, on the good side—they're responsible for the fertile soil on the hillsides. Crops like coffee and sugarcane grow in abundance. Then—pfft," he snapped his fingers, "an eruption takes place to change the topography, and the occupants of entire villages are driven out. That's bad. But the volcanoes are still beautiful and everybody affords them proper respect." His expression lightened as he recounted, "There was one called Izalco that faithfully erupted every three minutes for years. Navigators on Pacific waters even used it as a natural beacon. Then some developers erected a hotel to view the spectacle from Cerro Verde across the way. The building was no sooner completed than Izalco stopped, practically in midburst. There were no more eruptions. Naturally the hotel went broke." He shrugged. "The fates had a hand in it."

Laurel chuckled. "If you were in Hawaii, they'd say Madame Pele caused it—she's the goddess of volcanoes."

"I wish we were over there now," Elena put in. "At least something's happening in Hawaii. Not like here. And it will be worse when I get with my parents—they never let me do anything."

"Well, I wouldn't trade places with anyone right now," Laurel said emphatically. "Having El Salvador for a Christmas present is the greatest."

Elena made a moue of displeasure and searched through her purse to bring out her compact. "It would be better with Casey," she pronounced.

Laurel struggled to change the subject. "What are those trees in that field? They look like some kind of a crop."

"Bananas and papayas," Eduardo said, glancing out the bus window. "You'll find plenty of those on the way to the capital. Along with fields of tobacco and pastures of Brahma cattle. This is a fertile area. You can see for yourself at the market in Sonsonate—it's the small town just ahead of us."

Laurel concentrated on looking as their driver eventually slowed and turned left down a crowded village street, blasting away on his horn to clear it of people and wandering animals.

There were a half-dozen blocks of tiny shops jammed together on the wide sidewalks before they came to the big central market area. Overhead a metal awning protected the merchants from a late morning sun which was beating down relentlessly. Most of the shops were closed in deference to the holiday like one with the sign *"Fotos Urgentes—Servicio día y noche"* over the doorway. Even so, the sidewalks were still crowded with vendors who displayed their fresh produce on rough wooden stands. Green and red peppers were a different kind of Christmas decoration, Laurel decided, but a nice one. Especially when flanked by a display of plump red tomatoes and shiny cucumbers, nestling atop radish plants.

"It's a good thing I've just finished breakfast," she told Eduardo. "Otherwise, I'd want to get off to sample the merchandise. Oh, look at those baskets! I wish we could stop."

"There isn't time if we get into San Salvador on schedule for our lunch," Eduardo explained. "Never mind, you can explore the markets there and I'll buy you a *coco-loco* if you're thirsty."

"What's a *coco-loco*?" Elena wanted to know.

"Rum, sugar, and some other things," Eduardo said evasively. "You should try the favorite drink here."

"Coffee?" Elena asked suspiciously.

"Not at all. Chilled hard cider. They use it in their cooking, too. *Gallo en chicha* is a specialty of the country—that's chicken cooked in cider," he translated for Laurel's benefit. "It's very good. So are their appetizers—*pupusas*—corn cakes filled with meat or cream cheese."

Laurel shook her head dolefully. "I wish you'd stop talking about food. I'll never last the course."

He consulted his watch as the bus cruised by the Sonsonate town square, stopped at an intersection, and then turned onto the main highway again. "It shouldn't be more than an hour until we reach the capital. There's only one stop on the way—a coffee-processing plant . . . and that doesn't take long."

She was surprised to find how quickly the time passed. As it was to the rest of the passengers—with the possible exception of Elena who experimented with different shades of lipstick on the ride—the lush greenery of the Salvadoran landscape was a source of delight. Tall fields of sugarcane ran for miles and then were suddenly replaced by plantations of highland rice and Indian cotton. Bananas and mangoes appeared in carload quantities along with zapotes and avocados on either side.

Traffic was heavy on the two-lane road and every few minutes, they would overtake the local passenger buses loaded so tightly that Laurel was surprised they could even run. Suitcases and bundles were roped onto racks on the roofs of the ancient vehicles. She wondered how the owners ever claimed their belongings and felt a moment's sympathy for the drivers who climbed up like mountain goats when baggage had to be delivered at the roadside stops.

Eduardo was peering over her shoulder when their own driver slowed. "Ah—just as I thought. This is the place where they dry the coffee. We'll get off for a few minutes so you can see it."

Once the bus door opened, the passengers obediently threaded their way down the aisle. Even reluctant ones like Gwen who was saying loudly that coffee didn't interest her but some fresh air did.

"I wonder if Casey's here, too," Elena commented, going down the aisle ahead of Laurel and Eduardo. She leaned over to look through the bus windows and then straightened. "I don't see the car," she said fretfully.

"It may be ahead of our bus," Eduardo said. "You'll see him at lunch anyhow, so what does it matter?"

"I don't know. Things are more exciting when he's around." She made a grimace of displeasure. "Coffee plantations with *turistas*. Ugh!"

Eduardo squeezed Laurel's elbow purposefully as he brought up the rear of the column. "That puts us in our place," he breathed in her ear.

"Well, I fully intend to enjoy it," Laurel told him as she started down the bus steps. "I've never seen anything like this before. Oooosh!" She hesitated as she felt the first blast of outside air. "My lord, it's hot!"

They walked to the edge of the road and stood waiting with some of the others for a break in the traffic so they could cross the busy highway. At their feet, a grimy white rooster was investigating grass clumps for food as he played truant from some farmer's hen house. Still farther along, she could see a donkey tethered under a tree at the roadside and two more chickens foraging for food beside him as he browsed.

On the far side of the highway, a low brick wall protected a flat drying area equal to several city blocks where coffee beans were spread out to dry. Workers in the white uniforms of the processing plant were using long wooden rakes to level some beans while other men were unloading bags from a truck. Nearby, a group of laborers carrying shovels walked toward a cement square close to the road where bags were stacked for emptying.

"That's one hell of a lot of coffee," muttered an elderly man next to Laurel. "I'd sure like to get over there and take some pictures." He looked impatiently up the road. "I think we'll just have to make a break for it."

Eduardo shook his head warningly. "No . . . not here. It's a good way to get killed. In this country, pedestrians *don't* have the right of way." He paused to let a heavily loaded truck belching dark exhaust smoke go speeding by. "Burros, yes . . . but not people. There'll be a chance to get across in a minute."

Elena was peering around the end of the bus as they waited. "There's a car pulling up behind us . . . it must be Casey. I'm going to see." She edged her way back through the tight group of people still clustered at the front of the bus. As they moved aside to make room for her, Laurel found herself abruptly propelled forward. At the same time, the poor rooster found himself trapped under their feet. He squawked in alarm and tried to get out. Unfortunately, the only escape route opened onto the highway and he fluttered past the front of the bus directly into the path of an oncoming car.

There were screams of warning and every eye was on him as the driver hit his brake and blasted on his horn. At the very instant the rooster tried to swerve desperately away from this new menace, Laurel felt a thudding blow against her back. She clawed to keep her balance and then sprawled full length out on the highway in the midst of dust, feathers, and burning rubber.

She could hear the horror-stricken shouts of the people behind her—then she felt the pain of contact with the rough cement surface and realized, sickeningly, that she couldn't escape if another car were bearing down.

As Laurel tried desperately to push up on her elbows, she felt her ankles grasped roughly. Seconds later she was yanked back through the crowd onto the shoulder of the road. Even as she felt the loosening of that iron grip, another car roared past on the highway—inches from where she'd lain. Then arms were lifting her upright and a babble of voices surrounded her.

"I'll take her." She heard Casey's brusque tones and knew from the feel of his arm around her that he'd been the one who'd pulled her from danger.

"Let's give her some air." Peg Purcell's brisk tone made the others give way. "Casey . . . maybe the bus . . . she should lie down."

"She can go in my car. It's right back here." He looked fleetingly down into Laurel's face, which was drained of every vestige of color, and swept her into his arms. "Okay with you?"

Laurel nodded, still not able to answer. The nausea that had surged upward when she heard the noise of that last car was starting to subside but, at that moment, she could only turn her face against his chest and try not to think.

Then she felt herself being gently deposited on the rear seat of a car and she opened her eyes again, thankful that this time the horizon was staying firmly in place. She looked out into a sea of anxious faces; Casey and Peg were by the door while Eduardo and Elena hovered behind them. A knot of concerned passengers stared silently from a discreet distance.

Laurel felt she had to do something before they started draping black wreaths over the car. She managed to smile and keep her voice steady. "I feel lots better, thanks. I'll be perfectly okay as soon as I get my breath back."

"No doubt about it." Casey turned to face the crowd behind him. "Everything's under control here. Better go take your pictures. But be careful crossing that damned road," he warned as they started moving off. "The next person might not be as lucky as Laurel." Then he beckoned to the driver and drew him a few feet away as he talked to him.

Laurel's eyes shifted to the roadside and her aching body stiffened when she saw the body of the white rooster limp and broken at the edge of the gravel shoulder.

Peg followed her glance. "Don't look at it and don't think about it," she advised. "Otherwise, my husband will have a real case on his hands and he doesn't need the business."

"She's right, *chica,*" Eduardo contributed, leaning past Peg's shoulder. He saw Laurel's confusion. "What is it now?"

"My purse . . . I must have dropped it."

"I have it," Elena said, pushing past Eduardo. "It was on the ground."

"Thanks." Laurel took it gratefully. "I should have a handkerchief somewhere." She indicated her grazed knees and torn stockings. "It will have to be spit and polish unless there's some place . . ."

"Use this for a stopgap," Casey said, coming up to the car in time to hear the last of her words. He pulled his clean handkerchief from his pocket and shoved it into her hands. "The doc can take care of the rest at the ship."

She took the handkerchief automatically. "What do you mean . . . back at the ship? I'm headed the other way."

"No, you're not." His voice was firm but not unkind. "My driver's all set to take you back." He jerked his head toward the front seat where the man was sliding behind the wheel. "Peg can go with you."

The doctor's wife was evidently expecting something of the kind because she got obediently into the back beside Laurel even as he spoke. "Of course. And the sooner we get going, the better."

"But this isn't necessary," Laurel argued. "There's no reason to spoil Peg's day. I'll be perfectly all right by myself."

"Peg can catch up with us later if she wants to," Casey said, slamming the car door. "You do what Doc tells you to." His expression shaded momentarily as he looked over to the woman beside her. "He's on duty today, isn't he?"

Peg nodded, her lips tight with displeasure. "He's okay."

Laurel thought Casey muttered something that sounded like "He damned well better be," before he turned and gestured to the driver.

"I could stay with Laurel," Elena said with fierce determination. "I'd rather do it than be on that silly bus."

Casey put a casual arm around her. "Maybe, honey, but your nursing talent's on the thin side. You can take the night shift when we get back. Go ahead, Juan. I'll see you later."

The driver nodded and pulled away. Laurel only had time to respond to Eduardo's wave before they were immersed in the other traffic on the highway.

"Here . . . give me that handkerchief." Peg was looking her over. "I'll be as gentle as I can, but there's still grit on those skinned knees."

Laurel pulled another handkerchief from her purse to dab at her torn palms. Looking up to see the driver's concerned face in the rear-vision mirror, she said reassuringly, "I promise not to bleed on your upholstery."

"No es importa, senorita. Senor Casey takes care of everything."

"Oh, lord!" Laurel put a stricken hand to lips. "I forgot . . ."

Juan let up on the accelerator and Peg paused in her cleaning process. "Forgot what?" the latter asked. "Do we go back? Although how you make a U-turn on this road . . ."

"No . . . no. I didn't mean that. I just forgot to thank him."

"Casey?" Peg asked as the car surged forward again. Her tone was amused. "He'll survive."

Laurel clamped down on her lower lip to keep it from trembling. "The point is—*I* wouldn't have. He pulled me out of the road, didn't he?"

Peg thought it over and then nodded slowly. "I guess he did. It happened so fast and there were so many people—I'm still not sure what happened. Anyhow, Casey will understand. You can say it all later. He would have been embarrassed if you'd mentioned it. Men hate emotional displays."

"You're right." Laurel rested her head against the back of the seat and closed her eyes. It seemed the safest way to keep the tears from spilling over now that reaction was setting in.

Even in her confused state, she was aware that Casey had kept severely aloof. Not for a single second was there any indication that he remembered the woman he'd held in his arms the night before. If Laurel had wondered about his feelings, now she had proof positive.

Despite her intentions, a tear overflowed and rolled down her dusty cheek.

Peg saw it and misunderstood the reason. She reached over to pat Laurel's arm comfortingly. "Chin up, honey. We'll be back at the ship in no time. George can give you something to help the wobblies."

Thanks to Juan's skillful driving, they were back alongside the gangway at the Acajutla pier in half the time it had taken on the tour bus.

Help came from all sides as soon as Laurel's condition was known, but it was left to the brawny boatswain to take charge. He'd seen her hobbling to the gangway steps and hurried down to intercept her.

"With your permission, ma'am," he said as he swung her up in his powerful arms. "Down to the surgery or her stateroom, Mrs. Purcell?"

"The surgery, please, Boats. I'll go ahead and tell the doctor."

"This is very nice of you," Laurel said shyly when Peg hurried up the gangway.

"No trouble, ma'am. Looked as if you could use some help." He spoke without effort; in fact, Laurel felt that he hardly noticed her weight even as he moved steadily up the steep gangway and through the corridor of the crew deck to punch the elevator button with his elbow. "The doc'll take care of you."

George Purcell was waiting for them on the deck above when the elevator door opened. His face was flushed but he was in full control of the situation. "Right on down to surgery, Boats," he directed. Then, he shook his head in mock displeasure at Laurel. "I hear you've been playing in the traffic. Fine thing . . . on a holiday, too."

Laurel managed to smile at him, but she was profoundly glad when they reached his office where Peg awaited them. The boatswain deposited her gently on the surgery table and was gone through the door before Laurel could start to thank him.

"Don't worry," the doctor told her, leaning over to examine her bruised legs. "Boats is a good man. You don't have to spell things out with him. Peg . . . get some soap and water so I can remove this grime. Right now, Laurel could substitute as a mineral deposit."

For the next half-hour, he worked with deft but gentle hands cleaning and treating her knees and scratched palms. Peg forgot her customary wise-cracking attitude as she assisted him, confessing to Laurel that she had been working in a hospital when she'd met her husband.

"She didn't know that I was looking for an unpaid assistant just then. Otherwise she'd have run in the opposite direction." George smoothed the edge of an adhesive bandage on Laurel's knee and straightened with a sigh. "There . . . I think you'll do. That tetanus shot I gave you will cause you some discomfort but it's best to be on the safe side. I'll be around if you have any problems later on." He helped her to sit up on the table and steadied her. "Take it easy—you're feeling the aftermath of shock now and it's no wonder. From what Peg told me, it was a nasty experience. You'll be better after you've rested," he went on, helping her down to the floor but keeping an arm around her. "Once I get you back to your stateroom, I'll give you something so that you'll sleep."

Laurel wanted to say that it was an awful waste of her only day in El Salvador, but found she was too tired to even make a token protest.

Peg kept close on their heels as the doctor assisted Laurel down the deserted hallway. Aside from the muted hum of the air-conditioning units, the entire length of the pool deck might have belonged on a ghost ship.

When they arrived at the cabin, Peg fished the key from Laurel's purse and opened the door. Laurel looked surprised to find her sofa bed neatly made up and waiting.

The doctor's wife explained, "Boats undoubtedly told Hal to have the room ready. It's hard to get ahead of the crew's grapevine. And handy in this case."

"Peg will help you into bed," the doctor said. He put an envelope of pills on the dresser after shaking out two in Laurel's hand. "Take those with water after you're horizontal. They act fast . . ." He grinned. "I don't want my wife to come back and find you stretched out in the middle of the floor."

"Peg doesn't have to check on me." Laurel felt it was time she made some sort of rcsponse to show she was capable of it. "Besides, she's going back to rejoin the tour. The driver's waiting for her."

"You needn't talk about me as if I'd already left," Peg said with some amusement as she emerged from the bathroom carrying a glass of water. "I've changed my mind. I'll be around here."

"That's crazy. I'm perfectly all right," Laurel insisted. "There's no reason for you to give up your day ashore."

"Simmer down, honey. It isn't any great sacrifice. I'd already decided that sitting next to Gwen and hearing about every television role she'd had in the last five years wasn't my idea of fun. At any rate, I spent a day in San Salvador on the last cruise."

Laurel stared at her doubtfully. "Are you sure?"

"Positive. Sightseeing can't compete with a cold shower and a nice quiet lunch with my husband. Afterwards, I intend to sit in the shade and sew some more jewels on my costume. If I don't cover the vital places, I'll be arrested for indecent exposure." Peg spoke casually but she kept a close watch on Laurel's drooping eyelids. She turned and met her husband's gaze as if to say, "I'll take over from here."

The doctor nodded, his expression suddenly stern. "Check with me in surgery, Peg, after you're finished. Make sure she follows directions."

The rest of the afternoon might never have existed as far as their patient was concerned. Once Laurel was in bed, she barely had time to think how smooth and cool the sheets felt against her aching body before the medication took effect and pulled her into a drugged, dreamless sleep.

Hours later, it was the faint strain of music drifting in from the corridor that nudged her back to full consciousness. She opened her eyes and took a minute to remember the reason for being in bed while it was light outside. Then she stretched lazily on the unyielding mattress and winced as her stiff muscles protested.

Slowly she pushed up on one elbow, glad to find that some twinges of pain were the only tangible reminders of her experience. Rinsing her face with cold water helped—so did brushing her teeth and combing her hair. When she donned a quilted peach robe over her pajamas and searched for her lipstick, she discovered Peg's note on the dresser.

> Have checked twice with George and we've decided you'll live. Order dinner when you wake up. George says no roaming around until tomorrow. Will call later.

Laurel smiled as she read it and then reached for the phone. Dinner was a welcome suggestion, and, from the way her midsection felt, far overdue.

The chief steward's office must have been alerted for her call because Rip was knocking on her cabin door barely ten minutes later.

"It's sure too bad that you're missing Christmas dinner in the dining room," he told her as he put a laden tray on the foot of her bed while he set up a makeshift table. "The fellows spent all afternoon decorating the place and it really looks pretty. They have those woven Christmas trees in all the windows," he went on, "the kind they make in Guatemala."

"I'll see the decorations tomorrow," Laurel assured him. "I'm just eating in my room tonight."

"Yeah, I heard you tangled with some pavement." He stopped removing covers from the food long enough to give her a frowning appraisal. "You don't look so great," he said, deciding to level with her.

"You should have seen me before," she joked, wishing that people didn't always think honesty was the best policy. Rip had merely confirmed what the mirror had already revealed. "All I need now is some food," she told him, "and that smells awfully good."

"Prawns, steak, and the trimmings." He gave the tray a final glance. "I hope I didn't forget anything. Just put the dishes out in the hall when you're finished. Hal will pick them up for me. I can't leave the dining room again," he added importantly.

"Fair enough. Thank you, Rip."

"Shall I take the 'Do Not Disturb' sign off your door when I leave?"

She looked up, astounded. "Yes . . . please. I didn't know it was there. Mrs. Purcell must have put it on."

Rip nodded and hurried out.

Dinner *did* help—there was no doubt about it. Laurel thoroughly enjoyed the tastefully arranged meal and had just decided to skip the plum pudding when there was a brisk knock at her door.

Even as she called "Come in," it opened and Casey appeared in the hallway. His tall frame seemed to dwarf the surroundings as he pulled up short. "I thought you'd be finished with dinner," he said accusingly.

"Well . . . I am. I was just going to put the tray out in the hall."

"I'll do it." He came forward and took it from her hands. "You didn't eat your dessert."

She was amused at his concerned tone. "No . . . but I'm having a second cup of coffee. Doesn't that count?" She gestured toward the thermos and cup and saucer she'd placed on the shelf under the porthole.

He muttered something incomprehensible before taking the tray out to the corridor and disposing of it, closing the door firmly behind him as he returned.

Laurel felt a strange weakness assail her and sat down on the edge of the bed. "I'll share my coffee. That is, if you don't mind a bathroom glass."

"No, thanks. I'll be eating dinner in a little while." He looked around the room impatiently, as if feeling confined in the small space. "Mind if

I sit down?" he asked, nodding toward the only chair.

"Of course not. I'm sorry . . . I guess I'm still not thinking straight." Laurel didn't admit that her fuzziness began when he walked in the door. In his formal uniform for the holiday festivities, he seemed more unapproachable than ever and she found herself wishing that she had spent more time on her own appearance. "I just woke up a few minutes ago," she said when the silence began to bother her. "I don't know what was in those pills George gave me but they're certainly lethal."

Casey merely nodded, watching her with unnerving concentration.

Laurel plunged on brightly. "I finally heard some music from upstairs or I'd still be sleeping," she informed him, wishing to heaven that he'd say something before she had to resort to discussing the weather.

He finally roused himself. "That must have been the orphans."

She frowned. "What orphans?"

"The ones that came from the Children's Home in Sonsonate to sing some Christmas carols. They're up in the lounge now eating meringues and ice cream. I'd have brought you one . . ." He flashed a brief grin. "Meringue, I mean—only they're dangerous to eat in bed."

Her lips curved in response. "You're so right. If they don't explode off the saucer, then your fork sticks in them."

"The youngsters weren't bothered. When I left, some were going back for thirds. Nice bunch of kids," he added casually. "Everybody on the ship wants to come and see you. I put them all off because Peg and George said everything was under control."

"They've been wonderful to me. I couldn't have had better care." She fiddled aimlessly with the belt on her robe. "Bringing those orphans aboard was a great idea—I'm sorry I missed their concert. The passengers must have loved them."

Casey nodded absently as if his thoughts were on something else. His next words confirmed it. "There's no way to be diplomatic about this. If you feel up to it, I'd like to hear what happened out there on the highway. One minute you were upright—the next you were laid out flat on the pavement." When she didn't say anything, he went on in a level tone, "I intend to find out what happened if I have to sit here all night."

She turned on him angrily at that. "Do you think I haven't wondered? Ever since you picked me up and put me back together again—it's been like a nightmare." Her glance pleaded with him for understanding. "It all happened so fast. We'd gotten off the bus and were jammed together waiting to cross the highway. Then . . ." She had to steady her voice before she could go on. "I'm sure someone shoved me, Casey—but I don't know whether it was deliberate. That's what makes it so . . . damned difficult." The last sentence came out in a husky undertone.

He was up in an instant, bending over her. "Don't cry, honey." His hand smoothed a lock of hair back from her colorless face. "I'm a dirty dog to browbeat you." He sank down onto the edge of the bed beside her. "I guess I was hoping you'd say you tripped over a crack in the pavement."

"No such luck." If he hadn't withdrawn his hand by then, she would have leaned over and started howling on his immaculate shoulder. She took a deep breath and forced herself to ask, "Was it coincidence, Casey, or am I losing my mind? Why would anyone be after me?"

He rubbed his face wearily. "You work for Marden. On this trip, you've worked with me. Maybe that's enough. Unless you have any skeletons buried or disappointed lovers . . ."

"You make it sound like Gilbert and Sullivan. Probably by tomorrow this will all seem like a case of overworked imagination." She reached for a pillow and pushed it behind her back. "You'd better take the other one," she advised Casey. "These divan-beds aren't the last word in comfort."

He gave her a wry glance and then got to his feet. "No, thanks. It'll be safer if I put a respectable distance between us. Very compromising things . . . beds." His grin was slow in coming. "And tonight you're too bushed to fight back."

"That isn't funny . . ."

"It wasn't meant to be." He moved over to the hallway and shoved his hands in the pockets of his black dress uniform trousers. "Doc sent word that you're to take two more pills," he went on in a level tone. "You're also to leave your door unlocked. Peg will check on you later and Elena will come in if you want anything during the night. Now I'd better get going. If I don't make dinner on time one night this week, Miss Scott will be complaining to the captain."

"I still haven't thanked you for pulling me out

of danger." She was determined to finally say it. "You probably saved my life."

"Don't start fitting me for any halos," he said brusquely, staying where he was in the hallway. "You've known me long enough for that. My intentions are still strictly dishonorable."

Color washed across her pale cheeks. "I thought we'd settled that last night."

"We didn't settle a damn thing and you know it. All we did was postpone the final reckoning. If you weren't under the weather right now, this visit would be going along different lines." He frowned as he stared at her. "Do you think it's been easy for me—knowing you were alone in this cabin night after night. I've had a devil of a time staying away. That should amuse you," he added bitterly.

"Please, Casey—there's no point in talking about it . . ."

He went on as if she hadn't spoken. "If you weren't a stubborn coward, you'd admit that you want me to stay. Even now."

"I'm admitting nothing. I don't intend to. After last night's experience, I've decided to keep out of your way."

"And use Eduardo for light relief? I saw that little episode in the lounge. Be careful that you don't get caught in some deeper currents."

"Eduardo's been a perfect gentleman." Her chin took on a stubborn line. "Which is more than I can say . . ."

"About me? I told you not to fit me with any halos." He strode to the door but paused with his hand on the knob to look back at her slight form hunched on the side of the bed. His rugged features softened perceptibly. "You'll feel better in the morning, Laurie. Get some rest now . . . there's time to go into this later."

She sat without moving for a long time after he closed the door behind him. Then she turned on the bed and rested her forehead against the cool glass of the porthole, staring blankly into the water churning past as a tug nudged them toward the open sea.

Casey had no sooner disappeared from sight than she had wanted to run after him and call him back. Just like Miss Scott or Gwen Harper, she decided despairingly and could have pounded her fist against the wall for being such a fool. She should have known that a self-professed scoundrel was always the most fascinating of men, challenging any red-blooded woman to do her damndest to reform him.

Why couldn't she be thinking about Eduardo, who deserved kind thoughts? Or the man she'd been dating in San Francisco whose image had faded so that now she could hardly remember what he looked like. All because of a chief purser who added up his conquests as casually as other men totaled a bowling score!

Laurel sighed and lay back on her pillow. It was disconcerting to learn that falling in love was such an uncomfortable business. Not that it seemed to bother Casey in the least. Too bad that Dr. Purcell couldn't prescribe some special "behavior modification" pills for him, so he'd not be such a menace to unsuspecting females.

She slid down between the sheets and turned her head on her pillowcase, trying to find a cool spot. In that instant she could see Casey's image very clearly. Just before her eyelids fluttered and drowsiness finally overcame her, she knew that she didn't want his behavior changed at all. The only thing she wanted right then was to have him stretched out close beside her . . . ruthlessly ignoring all her protests before he went about the serious business of making love.

Chapter Six

When Laurel made her way up on deck the next morning, she found that her brief moment in the public eye had faded and that she had been replaced as the chief topic of conversation by the schools of glistening flying fish who took off from the bow waves and skimmed the top of the water all around the ship. Passengers and crew alike were fascinated by their antics and half the ship was hanging over the rail at the breakfast hour.

For the one or two curious souls who inquired after her health, Laurel told them truthfully that she was practically as good as new, other than harboring some battle scars. She didn't add that her main problem was a thing apart and that she planned to take doses of him very sparingly for the rest of the voyage.

That day it turned out to be easier than she'd hoped. Casey left her alone for her typing duties even to the extent of taking all his meals in the officers' mess. The latter information came from Eduardo who had saved a place for her beside him at the deck lunch.

"One of his assistants is sick, so Casey's snowed under. I met him coming out of the purser's office down on the pool deck . . . said he'd be hard at it until we get to Buenaventura three days from now."

"That's the port in Colombia, isn't it?"

He nodded and broke off a piece of roll. Picking up his knife to butter it, he pointed the end of it toward her to emphasize his words. "If you ask me, Casey has more than cargo on his mind."

Laurel felt her heartbeat quicken. "What makes you think so? Did he say anything?"

"No . . . but you can't go by that. Casey's cagey about leaking news." Eduardo chewed reflectively and then went on. "A chief purser has to be, since he deals with both passengers and crew."

"Then what makes you think something special's happening?"

"Simple. I heard two of the deck hands talking when I was sunning by the pool this morning. When you wouldn't come swimming with me," he added pointedly.

"Bruises don't do a thing for bikinis," she told him, "but go on with your story."

"Apparently Captain Samuels threw a surprise inspection below decks this morning. Afterwards, the chief officer told the crew they could expect more—especially after we leave Buenaventura."

"Why Buenaventura? I thought it was mainly a coffee port."

"It is, but these days the real money is in cocaine smuggling. Major rings operate in Peru and Bolivia but the stuff is funneled into Colombia for shipment to the U. S. market. That's why any ship that calls in at Buenaventura as well as Lima is under surveillance. That means trouble with the Customs officials and special searches later on. It all plays havoc with docking schedules. Marden can't afford it."

"I suppose it affects shippers like you, as well."

"Sim." He grimaced. "It eventually adds to the costs and we have to pay."

"How do smugglers hide the cocaine? On a ship of this size, I mean?"

"Take your pick." He waved a hand toward the deck below. "They can put it in the coffee cargo—plastic bags of contraband can be shoved in the center of the bags of beans," he explained when she looked puzzled. "Officials have even found it stuffed in frozen carcasses of beef. The possibilities on a ship this size are endless." He leaned back in his chair and reached for his glass of iced tea. "There's always something. Ten years ago the big market was heroin. Today it's cocaine. Tomorrow it may be gem stones . . . wherever there's the biggest pay-off for the risk involved. But that's enough of such talk."

She smiled. "The doom-and-gloom routine? First introduced by television commentators and editorial writers. I must say, I haven't missed them on this trip."

"Nor I." He flicked a finger at the Good Morning sheet which she had typed earlier. "Tonight I see we have a Casino Night. Will you be there?"

" 'Fraid not. Dr. Purcell insists I have to go to bed early. Otherwise, I'd not be in shape for the costume party and talent show tomorrow night."

"And you can't miss that because we're serving as judges," he said smugly.

She stared at him. "How did you know? I just received a note from the captain when I went to my stateroom before lunch."

"Casey is not the only one who has his methods. You didn't plan to compete for a prize, did you?"

"Heavens, no. Most of the women have been working on their costumes for days during Peg's class sessions. And I have no talent whatsoever."

"Precisely." He sat back and grinned at her. "Therefore we should be excellent critics. That is what I told the captain."

She started to laugh. "Are we the only ones judging?"

"No. The Countess makes the third. Her talent is of a different kind." He shook his head as Laurel started to laugh. "Forget that I said it. That's the trouble with shipboard life—it brings out the worst in us. Someone once said that 'Being on a ship was like being in jail, with the chance of being drowned.' Today I'd believe it."

"That doesn't sound like you, Eduardo."

"No?" He used his napkin and then tossed it carelessly on the table. "I think I'm about to rejoin the human race after seven years of running away from it. Since meeting you, Laurel, I've found that I'm just as vulnerable to a woman's appeal as any other man. That was an indulgence I thought I'd put behind me. Don't look so stricken . . ." he added softly and reached over to cover her hand on the table. "I'm also talented at reading between the lines—both in Brazilian and English—and I know when there's no hope." He turned her hand over and traced his finger down the palm. "You seem to be having trouble with your heart line. Is that right?"

She freed her fingers gently and dropped her hand to her lap. Despite Eduardo's kindness, she had no intention of discussing her troubles with

Casey. "You sound like the man who writes verses for fortune cookies. I refuse to furnish any material."

He nodded as if her evasive answer satisfied him. "I thought as much. Next time, we should travel by air. It's difficult to get involved on a 747. Between filling out Customs forms, balancing trays on your lap, and trying to order a drink before the movie, it's impossible to fall in love with the person sitting next to you on the aisle."

Laurel smiled and put her own napkin on the table as she stood up. "I'll remember. In the meantime, would you like to sit in a deck chair somewhere and stare at the horizon with me?"

"If we're behind a lifeboat or a pillar. I don't feel like making polite conversation."

She nodded gravely. "That sounds like just what I had in mind."

The next day followed much the same pattern. Late in the afternoon, Laurel caught a glimpse of Casey when she passed the bridge. She was sure that he saw her and lingered by the rail, giving him ample opportunity to come out and talk to her. After five minutes of staring over the side pretending to be fascinated by the swells, she was annoyed to find that he had disappeared by means of the inner stair. She marched on down to her cabin to get ready for dinner, flaying herself mentally every step of the way.

She dressed carefully in a floor-length dress of red lace and added its matching long-sleeved bolero jacket to hide her remaining scratches. When she sailed out in the hall, Hal whistled admiringly as she passed the linen room door.

"You look prettier than the ornament on top of the Christmas tree," he said fervently.

"That's just what I needed to hear," she assured him and went up to dinner feeling that life had some compensations after all.

The next hour and a half in the dining room put her newfound optimism to the test since Rip had one of his more difficult nights. When he finally arrived with dessert and coffee, Peg shook her head. "I'll never get changed into my costume if I don't go now," she explained, apologizing. "We're the last ones in the room. Everybody else is down getting dressed for the party."

"I don't know why you bother," her husband grumbled, still annoyed over his dinner. "Stick around and have coffee. You can't compete with the passengers anyway."

"After sewing on all those beads, I'm certainly going to at least wear the thing," she told him. "Besides, the captain prefers to have everyone take part. You'd better snap it up," she added to Laurel. "Casey likes things to start on time."

Laurel stared after her with a worried look and turned inquiringly to Eduardo.

"I intend to have coffee," he said firmly. "Casey can soothe people's feathers if they get impatient. Besides, we'll need our strength."

"What do you mean?"

"He means," Dr. Purcell said, shoveling sugar into his coffee, "that the talent contest on cruise ships strikes a new low in the annals of entertainment. If Ziegfeld had ever sat through one, he would have changed his line of work the minute he set foot on land. The last cruise there was a woman who played a flute solo . . ."

"There's nothing wrong with that."

The doctor raised a thick eyebrow. "Dressed in a get-up of turkish towels while she pulled a toy snake from a laundry basket with a string on her toe?"

Laurel swallowed. "Well, it's certainly different."

"You can say that again. But even *she* couldn't compete with a retired banker who appeared in a pink satin ballet costume and tennis shoes. Damned if he didn't dance 'Swan Lake' accompanied by a double Scotch and soda." The doctor's shoulders heaved with laughter. "And he didn't even remember it the next day. He went around asking who laced his shoes with pink ribbons."

"You've convinced me," Eduardo said. "More coffee?" he asked Laurel.

"By all means." Her eyes sparkled with laughter. "But let's not take long. I'd hate to miss anything."

When they finally moved into the lounge, they found a scene of pleasant pandemonium. At the end of the room, the organist was playing at full volume for an enthusiastic audience dressed in some of the strangest garb Laurel had ever seen.

The Christmas tree had been moved into a corner for safety and the spotlights formerly trained on it were now focused on a net of balloons suspended from the ceiling. A few hardy souls were attempting to dance under them, but most of the passengers were standing around waiting for the festivities to begin.

Casey met Laurel and Eduardo in the middle of the noisy room. "Cutting it a little fine, weren't you? The natives are getting restless." He jerked a thumb toward two empty places where Luisa was ensconced next to the organ. "That's your bailiwick. The prizes are on the table and the categories for awards are listed on a piece of paper. The talent contest comes first and the organist's all set with their numbers." He spared a minute to inspect Laurel as if she were in competition. "You look as if you're feeling better. George told me you were. There's a shindig up in the captain's day room after this—I'll talk to you about it later." With that, he nodded brusquely and took his leave.

"Well!" Laurel felt as dazed as if she'd just come through a tornado. "Does any of that make sense to you?" she asked Eduardo.

He steered her toward their places. "Oh, yes. At least the part about the contest. We'd better get started. *Como está,* Luisa? May we join you?"

"You'd better," the Countess informed them. She was dressed in a gown of green net with a decolleté neckline which flattered her tanned shoulders. "Casey just muttered something about prizes and stalked away. He's like a bear these days." While she spoke, the Countess let her glance wander over Laurie's gown. "Nice," she said finally and nodded. Then she raised her glass of champagne just as a waiter served the other two. *"Viel Glück!* Tonight we'll need more diplomacy than a U. N. ambassador."

Laurel cast a nervous glance around the lounge. Even with the noise and bustle, there was a waiting expectancy and a good many eyes were already on the judges' table.

"Luisa's right—" Eduardo broke off as the organist signaled attention with a series of chords. A third purser dimmed the lights and brought a microphone into the middle of the dance floor ready for the competitors in the talent contest. "Remember," Eduardo said close to Laurel's ear, "look enthusiastic no matter how horrible it is. Have some more champagne—that helps."

His warning came just in time as the first entrants hove into view, made up as an Indian brave and his squaw. Identification was easy in the man's case because of the feather headdress on his bald head and the war paint streaked over his bare chest. Unfortunately, his wife didn't fare as well in the costume department; her overweight figure wasn't flattered by the jeweled crepe-paper shift that she fondly imagined Hiawatha might have worn.

Eduardo stared in fascination at the bulging outlines of her figure. "In America, you'd say she has a chest," he muttered with awe, "but in Brazil we'd say she has a wardrobe."

Luisa choked on her champagne and had to be pounded on the back but fortunately the Indians didn't notice. They were too busy launching into a rendition of the "Indian Love Call" that was a greater indignity than the happenings at Wounded Knee. Their voices rose with a fervor that made the young purser leap to shut off the microphone.

The competition went on and on and on. The quality standard was abysmally low but there was an abundance of enthusiasm and sheer goodwill. By the end of the program, Laurel found herself almost weak with laughter as she applauded.

In the costume party following, the judges decided that Elena should be given first prize for originality after she appeared as "Miss Lifeboat Drill" or "Ready for Anything." Her long hair was up in curlers and her face glistened with night cream as she showed the latest in unofficial emergency garb. She wore a bright orange life jacket over short cotton pajamas but instead of the brimmed hat and warm blanket that Casey recommended she had made a few substitutions . . . a bottle of champagne was clutched in one hand, an inflated inner tube in the other, and tucked providentially in the belt of her life vest was a copy of *Lady Chatterley's Lover* (in Spanish). Two chocolate bars and a bottle of Chanel #5 completed her display plus a tiny first aid box which dangled beside the whistle on her life jacket.

Peg Purcell won the prize for the prettiest costume in her belly dancer's outfit with blue and green "jewels" sewn over the halter and harem trousers.

She told them happily as she accepted the prize, "I have a million more things to sew on, but maybe I can get it finished before the northbound trip."

Luisa stared after her when Peg went to rejoin the doctor. "That woman has talent. She could make a living with her needle, if necessary."

Eduardo was staring at the doctor's flushed face. "If George keeps devoting his nights to a bottle of cognac, she may have to. One thing sure, he'll never make the party later." He put down his pencil and surveyed the bare table top in front of them as the organist slid into "I Left My Heart in San Francisco" to signal the end of the costume event and the beginning of dancing. "Thank God, that's over. Most everybody seemed to agree with our decisions."

"Not Miss Scott," Luisa observed. "I think she expected a prize for her 'Amazon monkey' routine."

"Jeans and a work shirt don't make much of a costume and climbing on the furniture doesn't take talent," Laurel put in.

"You must admit she *looked* like a monkey. That should count for something," Eduardo said solemnly. "One day she's going to comb her hair and nobody'll recognize her."

Luisa was staring through the crowd. "Right now, she's drowning her disappointment in champagne. It doesn't sound like a bad idea. We might as well go on up to the captain's day room for ours."

Eduardo shrugged but stood as she got to her feet. "The music's good," he said. "We could dance a bit first."

"Exactly what I had in mind," Ted Jensen said, moving over beside them. His chief officer's dress uniform looked more starched and immaculate than usual. The reason became evident when he went on to say, "I just arrived at this shindig. Since I missed all the program, I think I deserve a little consolation."

Luisa smiled but shook her head. "I'm on my way up to the captain's day room. Sometimes the steward forgets about the hors d'oeuvres and ordering that special bourbon that Gwen likes. I'll see you all later." She picked up her purse, gave them a brisk little nod, and moved toward the door.

"No, you don't!" Jensen put an arm around Laurel's waist when Eduardo would have pulled her out on the dance floor. "I'm pulling rank this time. The chief officer may lose out to the captain but never to a passenger. Besides, now that Elena's shed that costume, she's coming this way and your Spanish is better than mine," he told the Brazilian.

Eduardo gave him a sour look but stepped back. "That's the trouble with American ships," he advised Laurel half-seriously. "Fraternizing between the officers and the passengers would never be allowed anywhere else. People like Ted wouldn't get off the bridge."

"On foreign ships, the officers invite the ladies up *on* the bridge," Jensen countered before he grinned and swept Laurel away. "This is what I had in mind all along," he said as they circled the floor. "The Countess pulled age and rank on us."

"I didn't mind. She's really very nice. Too nice to . . ." Belatedly Laurel realized where she was headed and her voice trailed off.

"To be playing unofficial hostess while she's on board?" The chief officer's tone was matter-of-fact. "It's not worth bothering your head about. There are always risks when a man and woman don't follow convention—but maybe they think it's worth it. Their relationship isn't necessarily cheap or shoddy," he added. "They know the rules."

"Which are?"

"That it all ends when we tie up again at our home port. The first commandment of a shipboard romance. I'm surprised it isn't posted on the stateroom walls along with the emergency procedures." His face brightened as the organist segued into a fast rhumba. "Ah, that's my kind of music. Let's show these folks how it's done."

After that, Laurel scarcely had time to breathe, let alone dwell on his remarks about casual shipboard romances. Like Casey, he seemed to think it was the normal state of affairs at sea. Her lips curved as she thought about the phrase "state of affairs." It fitted the *Traveler* better than any advertising copy.

Ted regretfully relinquished her at the end of the Latin-American set and she danced the next group with Eduardo who was complaining about a dance floor littered with sheiks, human Christmas trees, and overweight American-type Indians. "Hiawatha ran into me during that last tango and I thought I'd never move again." He held up his scuffed shoe to illustrate. "Do you suppose she was a lady wrestler before he married her?"

"I heard she was a social worker."

"No wonder there are so many juvenile delinquents in southern California." He pulled Laurel from the path of a couple determinedly waltzing to a fox trot. "Have you had enough of this scrum? By now, I'm ready for Luisa's hot hors d'oeuvres and the captain's Scotch." He looked around the room. "Elena and Gwen are missing . . . so's Casey. They must have gone ahead."

For no reason, Ted Jensen's words "it all ends when we tie up again at home port" flashed through Laurel's thoughts. The prospect of Gwen hovering over Casey in the meantime didn't lend any enchantment.

"Somewhere I've picked up a headache," she said, rubbing her head to add conviction. Suddenly she realized that it was true and her voice gained strength. "I'll skip the party this time . . ."

"But you skip them *every* time." Eduardo's

stormy countenance showed what he thought of the new development. "You're worse than some Cinderella. At least she stayed around until midnight. Now it's only eleven thirty," he added accusingly, consulting his watch. *"Dios!* Tonight they might even have a real midnight buffet."

She smiled at his amazement. "It's almost worth waiting for. Well, maybe another time ..." She turned and led the way through the dancers to the end of the lounge.

"For you, I'd skip the party," Eduardo said, following closely. "We could dance and wait for the balloons with prizes. If Casey *has* any prizes left to give."

Laurel didn't want to pursue that subject either. She paused at the head of the stairs and said, "Not tonight, thanks. I hope you enjoy the party, though. See you in the morning, Eduardo." She blew him a kiss and hurried down the stairs. At the bottom, she almost collided with a uniformed figure hurrying up. "You!" she said in dismay to the chief purser. "I thought you were up at the captain's party with Gwen."

He drew back to rake her with his glance. "Which is why you're scurrying back to your hole like a good little mouse, I suppose. Well, you were wrong. I don't have time for any partying tonight. There's been a dust-up with a couple of the crew."

"Was anyone hurt?"

He shook his head. "Nothing serious. We stopped it in time." He started to move on, then paused and added, "I could use your help tomorrow with the Neptune crossing. Somebody has to handle the makeup for the pirates."

"Of course." Laurel tried to control the disappointment in her voice. Somehow she hadn't thought that the next encounter with Casey would find them discussing anything so mundane.

Casey's wry smile showed he was reading her thoughts again. "You can't have it all ways, you know. Sooner or later, you'll have to make up your mind."

"I don't know what you're talking about."

"The hell you don't. Incidentally, don't make any plans for Buenaventura."

"Why? What's up?"

"I was just talking to the main office." He gave a hasty look at his watch and swore softly. "I don't have time to explain now. Stop by the day room tomorrow about eleven and I'll explain before the makeup session."

"What about the Good Morning sheet?"

"I'll have one of the crew type it. If I keep using you for free, you'll complain to the main office. Of course, I *could* make it worth your while . . ."

"Good *night*, Mr. Waring."

His nod was just as brief. "Good night, Miss Cavanaugh. Phone the night steward for another blanket if you get cold in bed." He was gone up the stairs before Laurel could snarl a reply.

Chapter Seven

Casey opened the door to his day room promptly after Laurel's knock the next forenoon. "Come on in . . . and take that look off your face," he said when she stepped back in surprise and started to laugh.

"That black robe should be in a horror movie or a Salvation Army barrel," she said, still laughing. "What are you . . . the Wicked Witch of the North?"

"Certainly not. Don't you recognize an English prosecutor when you see one?" He sighed, "The damn fool things a man does to earn a living . . ."

"Prosecutor for whom?" Laurel persisted, intrigued.

"King Neptune, of course. Today's the trial of the polliwogs at the Crossing of the Equator ceremony. The passengers would stage a mutiny if we ignored it." He pulled off the long advocate's wig which reached the shoulders of his academic gown. "This outfit's hotter than the fringes of hell but at least it's better than the King's costume. His robes weigh a ton."

"Who's taking the part of King Neptune?"

"The third mate." Casey shrugged out of his

robe and stood before her in khaki shorts and a white T-shirt. "He's done it before."

"Did he volunteer for the job?"

"Not exactly." Casey grinned as he went over to pour two cups of coffee from an insulated carafe on the desk. "But he's off duty and has a beard so he was shanghaied into the role. Actually everybody has a good time and most of the fellows who are off duty come up to watch." He gave her the coffee and motioned her toward a chair. "The actual equator crossing is between Colombia and Peru but it's more convenient to hold the shindig now."

"You'd better give me a rundown so I'll know what to do."

He looked surprised. "You've been across the line, haven't you? I had you listed as a shellback." A wicked glint came into his eyes. "You mean you're just a lowly polliwog after all?"

"Nope." Her expression was just as mocking as his. "Find another victim. I've been across—but never on a ship."

"Flying doesn't really count," he informed her, "but I'll have to overlook it in your case. I need all the help I can get. Half the passenger list has signed up as polliwogs."

Laurel took a sip of coffee and made herself comfortable. "What do you do to them?"

"Read out all their crimes—present them to the King and Queen and then turn them over to the Royal Barber—that's Eduardo—who'll add a few final touches before we push them in the pool."

She gave him a suspicious look. "What kind of touches?"

"Raw eggs in their hair, ice cubes down the

back of them, red dye down the front . . . a string of dead fish around their neck and a cup of flour tossed over the whole thing."

"You can't mean it!"

"I certainly do. The polliwogs wear swim suits or their oldest clothes and have a fine time. Of course the pool has to be drained afterwards . . . the water gets a little thick."

"Do all the passengers who haven't crossed the equator have to take part?"

"Lord, no. Just the ones who want to. That's where you come in. After you put greasepaint on the shellbacks in their pirate costumes, I want you to hang around the pool and make sure that only the right people go in the water. Sometimes the pirates get a little carried away."

"That sounds simple enough."

"I know. That wasn't the real reason I wanted to talk to you." He saw her instinctive withdrawal and frowned. "There's no need to be so suspicious. I seldom make passes at women before noon."

"Unless they're complaining about stuck drawers or something like that." The words were out before she could stop them and she flushed at his reproving look.

"Have some more coffee," he urged. "You're beginning to sound feline. I'd hate to have you suffer from pangs of conscience on my account. On the other hand"—he stretched out more comfortably on the small settee—"it's probably good for you to talk about it. I've suspected all along you were repressed but I didn't know you were a cynic as well."

She held onto her temper with an effort. "The

word is skeptic. And the symptoms only emerge when I'm around you."

"Like pollen attracting a honey bee," he murmured, pleased.

"More like pollen and a hay-fever sufferer," she corrected.

"Well, at least I've made some impression on you. I'd hate to admit utter failure. It does things to a man's ego. I just wish you'd dress in keeping with those stiff-necked philosophies of yours." He was eyeing her snug-fitting patchwork slacks and V-necked blouse irritably. "That outfit doesn't go with the image."

His words were inexpressibly soothing to Laurie. Apparently she was doing something right, after all. She dropped her lashes but managed to survey him thoroughly in the process. He looked tired, she decided. There were lines of fatigue at the corners of his eyes which hadn't been there at the start of the voyage. As if something was worrying him . . . or somebody.

That possibility made her day brighter. There was nothing like tangible evidence that she wasn't suffering alone.

"Did you hear what I said?" he growled.

"Absolutely. I'll go through my wardrobe as soon as I get back to my cabin. There must be some sackcloth someplace. Was there anything else you wanted to tell me?"

"I haven't told you anything yet." He was scowling at her like a man fast approaching the end of his patience.

"It's just as well. You know what happened to Socrates when he went around giving people advice."

"If I'd known you were going to be like this, I'd have asked for a side order of hemlock when I called for the damned coffee," he snarled. "Could you pipe down and pay attention for a few minutes?" He got up and strode over to refill his cup. "Maybe it's just as well I'm going away for a few days."

His sudden announcement wiped all the levity from Laurel's face. "I . . . I didn't know," she said finally. "Are they taking you off the ship?"

"Not officially. We dock in Buenaventura late tonight. Unfortunately we just stay in port part of the day tomorrow before we leave for Lima. There've been some new court decisions down here on drug smuggling. I have to go inland to talk to the officials at Calli. I'll rejoin the ship at Lima a couple days later."

"I see." Laurel stood up and went to stare out the porthole. "Where do I fit in?"

"I need your help to scout a possible shore excursion out of Buenaventura. The tour people there have come up with an all-day package . . . it involves a trip on a launch up the Agua Dulce River and visiting an Indian village in the jungle. You'll have to find out if the facilities are satisfactory for food and possible overnight accommodation. I've asked Peg to go along with you. Does it sound okay?"

"Of course." She turned to face him. "But I should warn you that I don't know a darned thing about jungle tribes or their way of life."

"That's okay." He smiled slightly. "Actually, this is one time when knowing nothing is an asset. The main thing is whether the average cruise passenger would enjoy this outing. If you're in doubt about anything on the Indian menu, for pete's sake, don't eat it." His glance lingered on her, noting how the sunlight streaming through the porthole made a shining golden halo on her brown hair. He almost mentioned it and then stopped abruptly. A halo on that particular feminine head was the very thing that had been causing him trouble all along. There was no sense dwelling on it.

Laurel heard him sigh and watched him put his cup back on the tray. "What about times and places? Where do I find their launch? Things like that."

"I'll leave a note on the desk with the details." He sounded tired of the whole thing. "Be prepared for plenty of heat and stock up on mosquito repellent."

"Will you still be around in the morning?" she asked, keeping a noncommittal tone.

"Probably not. If you have any questions, ask Peg. She has a working knowledge of Spanish, too—in case you need it."

"Oh, lord—I hadn't thought of that."

He yanked the door open. "Well, don't lose any sleep over it. You'll be fine. Not only that, you'll have a good story to tell when you get back home." Scooping up his robe and wig, he motioned her ahead of him out the door.

His expression was annoyed as she padded quietly along at his side on her way up the stairs to the Inca Lounge. For a minute there, he could have sworn she was dismayed by his news of leaving the ship. Then she'd retreated again behind the wall she'd so carefully erected between them ever since he'd held her in his arms that night up on the flying bridge.

Casey glanced irritably again at the delicate line of her profile when she pulled up outside the lounge door beside him. She felt his glance and turned to meet it squarely.

He gave way to his baser instincts. "I was thinking that it's a shame you'll have so little to remember on this trip. Just some pictures of a long boat ride and a bunch of friendly Indians."

She stared back at him warily. "What's wrong with that?"

"If we could have taken the shore trip together, it would have been a hell of a lot better." He saw that he had her attention and went on smoothly. "We could have found our own deserted island on the Agua Dulce—one with palm trees, soft breezes, not another soul around. How does that sound?"

She appeared to consider it. "I don't know. I've always heard that the ideal man to take to a deserted island was a good obstetrician." At his sudden scowl, she went on innocently, "Sorry, I didn't mean to annoy you . . . but what about mosquitos? I'm not at my best with them . . . and I do think that it helps if you take distilled water to a place like that. Otherwise, heaven knows what you can catch—" She broke off as he shoved open the lounge door with considerable force. "Oh! Are we going on in?"

"You bet. I've too much to do to keep on wasting my time." As she struggled to keep a straight face, he went on sourly. "You're right. It wouldn't work. I'd probably drown you in the Agua Dulce in the first hour."

After that, Laurel didn't find it hard to stay out

of Casey's way for the rest of the day. Since he seemed to be employing the same tactics, it was doubly easy.

The first thing Laurel noticed when she awoke the next morning was the cessation of movement. Since the weather had been almost perfect most of the voyage, she had long since taken the rhythmic up and down pattern of the *Traveler* for granted. It wasn't until they tied up at a pier that she was aware of the sudden quiet. Even then, it seemed as if the big ship were straining at her mooring ropes, anxious to be at sea again. Which, when it came right down to it, Laurel realized, was the way she felt, too.

After a quick look over the rail at the Colombian port on her way to breakfast, she was surer than ever. For one thing, it was hot at Buenaventura. Soggy, wilting, sticky, humid, without-a-breath-of-air heat that made the few individuals lounging on the pier hurriedly seek a shady spot. Most of them were leaning against the bags of coffee beans which were piled on pallets for loading. Otherwise, the pier was deserted and the barren expanse of concrete was simply an unattractive dusty slab.

Most of the town's activity seemed to be centered a good distance away from the dock. As Laurel looked past a block or so of untended vacant lots, she could see a line of trucks waiting for entrance at the port gates. Either the examination of their loads was a long one or the whims of South American officialdom didn't cater to morning work hours.

When Laurel made her way to the dining salon

a few minutes later, she found that the windows on the other side of the ship overlooked a more picturesque scene. The wide inlet where they'd anchored was bounded on the far side by gently rolling hills matted with tropical vegetation.

The overall vista might have been snatched from a Winslow Homer watercolor; the sky was the bright blue of equatorial latitudes, echoed in intensity by the vibrant greens of the hillside foliage. Only the color of the slow-moving water looked out of place; it was an unattractive shade of brownish gray suited only for making mud pies.

The few boatmen going past the *Traveler*'s hull didn't seem to mind. Two men were in worn dugout canoes and their nearly naked brown bodies blended in color with the water beneath the small craft. Another boatman had erected a patched sail and was sitting calmly on the edge of his canoe as it heeled precariously under a sudden puff of wind. A neatly painted launch with a powerful outboard shot into view alongside and disappeared just as quickly. Laurel tried to see where it was headed but lost it behind the containers still piled high on the *Traveler*'s bow.

"I hoped I'd find you here." Peg Purcell dropped into the chair beside her and made motions of pouring coffee to Rip who had just emerged from the galley. The doctor's wife looked comfortable in a pale blue sleeveless dress with her blond hair bound back in a matching scarf. She put her elbows on the table and dropped her chin in her palm. "Thank heavens for air conditioning. This blasted port is always stifling."

Laurel pushed her plate of sweet rolls aside.

"Casey warned me about it yesterday. That's why I put on this outfit—it's the coolest I own. Do you think it'll be all right for our trip?" She indicated her denim skirt and jacket which were brightened by a striped halter top. "I can take the jacket off if it gets too hot on the river." She frowned slightly as she surveyed Peg's outfit. "You look awfully dressy . . . maybe I should change."

"No." The word came out sharply. "That's what I wanted to talk to you about," Peg went on. "I'll have to leave you in the lurch today. George is . . . under the weather." The way she hesitated left no doubt as to the cause of the doctor's indisposition. "Casey will be furious, but if I stay around, maybe I can make sure the captain doesn't find out. This is George's last trip." Her voice was strained as she appealed to Laurel. "I can't have him sent home from Lima in disgrace. You *do* understand, don't you?"

"Of course . . . but . . ." Laurel bit her lip in confusion.

"What's the matter?"

"I'm just wondering if I should go alone. Without any Spanish and all. Maybe I should ask Eduardo . . ."

"No luck there. I heard him telling about a business appointment in town today. Of course, there's Elena . . . but she's awfully young."

Laurel shook her head. "I couldn't drag her into it. Casey didn't know what provisions they've made at the Indian village."

"Look—it needn't be too bad." Peg hunched forward as she spoke. "I'll put you on the launch and explain things to the boat man. Everything else can be done by sign language. After all, it's only for a few hours."

"I suppose you're right." Laurel was still reluctant. "Has Casey left the ship yet?"

"Yes, he was off first thing. About the time the Indians came aboard." Seeing Laurel's mystified expression, she explained. "The four Indians down by the swimming pool. They arrived early—complete with stacks of ponchos and blankets. A lot of the passengers prefer to shop on the ship in comfort. Besides," she added meaningfully, "Buenaventura isn't the best place to go ashore. You'll be a lot safer on your river excursion than wandering around town. At least, you won't have to take off your jewelry."

Laurel looked startled. "I didn't know it was like that."

"Well, it is." Peg took a last gulp of coffee and stood up. "When you're ready to go ashore, give me a call in the surgery. I'll take you to the launch and explain everything to the boatman. Don't forget a hat with a brim," she added. "The sun here can be brutal."

After she'd left, Laurel decided to take time for a final cup of coffee. Inwardly she acknowledged that she was simply stalling; the river excursion hadn't sounded very inviting even with Peg as a companion. Alone, it wasn't tempting at all.

When she made her way down to the dock a half hour later and found the tiny launch tied up aft of the *Traveler*'s stern, her worst fears were realized. Instead of the trim craft that Casey had mentioned, she was faced with a gondola-type excursion boat which bore a tattered awning amidships and peeling paint everywhere else. The only modern thing on it was the big outboard motor attached to the stern.

A thin individual in khaki shorts and a stained T-shirt bounded up the crude gangway as Peg came to join them on the dock. She addressed the boatman in halting Spanish and left Laurel to take a closer look at the craft below.

Two plank benches on the sides of the launch provided the entire seating space except for a small wooden box in the bow which doubled for storage. The boatman sat on a ledge by the motor at the stern.

"This doesn't make sense," Laurel said when Peg finally came back to join her. "You couldn't squeeze more than twelve passengers on this contraption. Even if they still wanted to go after seeing it . . . which I doubt."

"This isn't the regular launch. Apparently the boatman was having engine trouble with that one, so the tour company substituted this for the occasion. Better hop aboard."

"Are you sure he knows what I'm supposed to see?"

"I explained everything. He'll take you to the Indian village and then bring you back in the afternoon." Peg fanned her face with her open hand. "Lord, it's hot! I envy you . . . there should be a breeze on the river. Look, I really have to get back to George. The fool was bent on holding surgery hours when I left."

"Of course. Go ahead." Laurel managed a weak smile. "I'll see you when I get back."

"Thanks, honey. You're a brick to cover for me!" Peg squeezed her shoulder affectionately and hurried back toward the *Traveler*'s gangway. She had only taken a few steps when she stopped to call over her shoulder, "I forgot to tell you. The fellow's name is Estéban." She gestured in the general direction of the launch.

"Great," Laurel muttered to herself as she went cautiously down the gangway. "Some conversation we'll have, 'You Estéban—me Jane.' "

Estéban was waiting for her at the edge of the launch and put up a strong hand to help her aboard. It was soon apparent that the lack of a common language didn't daunt him. "*'Dias, senorita. Como está?*" He led her to the end of the bench as he rattled on. "*Siéntese, por favor. Solamente un momento—*" Suddenly it occurred to him that he wasn't getting through. "*Ahora, vamos.*" He accompanied the last with a sliding hand gesture and added a creditable outboard-motor noise for a clincher.

Laurel laughed, her apprehension fading. "Okay, Estéban, *vamos*. Any time, I'm with you all the way," she added as he grinned in response. Then he pushed the gangway aside and hurried to release the bow line before seating himself importantly in front of the motor.

A minute later, they zoomed out into the main current of water at a speed that had Laurie clutching the side of the launch to stay aboard. Estéban must have noted her distress, because he beamed reassuringly and cut his speed by half as he headed toward the Agua Dulce River.

After they passed the first bend of the wide waterway, they seemed to cut the last cord with civilization. Estéban chose to follow the bank of the river to avoid the stronger currents in the center, giving Laurel a chance to view the vegetation at close range. She was amazed to find how seemingly impenetrable it was and how desolate. On their entire journey, they didn't pass more than four or five huts erected on stilts by the river's banks. Usually two or three naked youngsters were playing nearby and occasionally a woman would wave from the open doorway. Subsistence gardens around the homes plus banana palms and pineapple plants showed that food wasn't a problem. Evidently close-knit family ties sufficed for a social life.

Later, the launch came alongside a long snake in the water and Estéban idled the motor so that they could watch its progress until it finally slithered up on a muddy spit. When their speed was cut, the slight breeze disappeared with it and the moist heat immediately made Laurel's halter top cling to her body. For an instant she thought of slipping her jacket over her shoulders and then discarded the idea as she felt perspiration dripping down her back.

Estéban finally turned off the motor about fifteen minutes later. *"Allí, senorita,"* he said, gesturing toward a crude pier extending from the gently sloping bank ahead of them.

Laurel nodded and smiled. Then as her gaze swept the deserted path which led into the undergrowth beyond the pier, a slight frown went over her features. She hadn't expected a royal welcome but she hadn't expected to be completely ignored either.

It turned out she needn't have worried. After Estéban tied up the launch with a couple of deft maneuvers, he turned to her.

"Yo," he said, pointing to himself, *"y la senorita . . ."*

Laurel gestured amiably. *"Yo."*

"Sí. Nosotros andamos." He hopped up to the pier and marched theatrically in place. *"A los Indios."* He peered at her for confirmation.

"Sí . . . sí . . . sí." She reached in her purse for her sun hat and put it on. Then she scrambled over to the other side of the launch and let him help her up on the pier. *"A los Indios,"* she repeated.

That time, Estéban's grin covered half his face. He turned and strode toward the path, but since he measured only an inch or two more than Laurel's five-foot-four, she had no trouble adjusting her steps to his.

A high-pitched whining noise in the air around them indicated that the mosquito brigade was out for a full-fledged welcome. They'd brought along their friends—some of the biggest flies Laurel had ever seen. She sent up silent blessings for her long-sleeved jacket and the mosquito repellent that she'd thought to apply earlier.

As they moved inland, Laurel found that the area was full of other living creatures. Clouds of birds fluttered in the trees overhead, swooping into the branches with a flash of color against the blue sky. Estéban gestured proudly toward them and then indicated a stream of ants which carried pieces of leaves and twigs as they moved beside the path in battalion strength.

Shortly after that, Estéban gestured toward some smaller red ants climbing on a tree trunk and pantomimed how their bite would poison a victim.

Laurel moved prudently back and nodded to show she understood. "What a way to go," she murmured. "I hope they don't come to our picnic lunch, too. It's going to be crowded enough with the mosquitos and the flies."

Estéban frowned. *"No comprendo, senorita."*

"That's all right. It wasn't important." She smiled and gestured on up the path.

After that, it was only a few more minutes before they emerged from the thick trees and vines into a clearing.

"Los indios," Estéban said importantly. He waved toward the group of people clustered around some palm-thatched huts. At the far side of the clearing, they could see a small European-type building with doors opening onto a broad screened porch. Between the two, some women were tending fires and cooking pots on a crude stove.

Laurel moved slowly forward at Estéban's side, trying not to stare at the colorful garb on the natives. The adult men wore only a type of raffia skirt which covered them from waist to mid-calf while the young boys settled for abbreviated loincloths. One toddler wore a miniature hula skirt and beamed on the two newcomers as he wobbled on uneven sod.

Two women, their long black hair held back by raffia headbands, approached shyly. The others, clad only in brown fiber skirts, stayed by the stove where lunch was in preparation.

As the two women gestured to her, Laurel looked around to Estéban for confirmation and saw that he had joined a group of men. The Indians spoke in some kind of dialect that carried across the still air and then nodded as Estéban gave some orders.

"Senorita!" His call made her glance apologetically to the two women who were urging her toward the stove.

"Sorry," she mouthed and went toward him. By then, he had taken up a place alongside a wigwam made of poles which could be covered with palm mats for protection from the weather.

Four of the natives had assembled nearby, each carrying a blowgun fully nine feet long. Gourds containing the darts for ammunition were suspended from their necks by raffia cords.

Before Laurel could get the wrong idea, Estéban performed another charade indicating that the men would aim for a tree at the clearing edge. After Laurel watched the first round, she decided Wild Bill Hickok didn't have to worry about his laurels. While handling a blowgun certainly required some skill, the demonstration definitely palled after ten minutes in the hot sun.

Fortunately, her hosts' enthusiasm waned as rapidly as Laurel's. The next time they recovered their darts from the tree trunk, they disappeared prudently into the background as the sound of a thready tom-tom was heard. A few minutes later, three more men sashayed apathetically into the clearing for a native dance.

That their routine was old hat was confirmed when even the toddler took one look and departed to admire a pet monkey which, in turn, was admiring the lunch at close range.

Laurel had just congratulated the youngster on his good sense when she heard some heavy breathing nearby. Estéban had moved to sit in a shady spot. His eyes were now closed and his mouth was open.

Laurel debated following his example and then remembered the ants and stayed reluctantly where she was. Just when she thought that she couldn't stand one more war dance, the men moved offstage and Estéban came amazingly awake.

"Ahora, senorita ... pronto, por favor." He pointed to the stove. Lunch was lunch, and it didn't need translating that he intended for them to be first in line.

When the entree was ladled onto a chipped plate and handed to her, Laurel remembered Casey's warning and wished to heaven that she could claim a rain check. The stew looked strange and smelled stranger. She poked Estéban to get his attention, pointed at the misshapen chunks, and raised her eyebrows inquiringly.

Estéban gestured happily toward the red-faced monkey which now watched them cannily from the edge of the porch. Apparently he had not come to the Indian village as an only child.

"Oh, God," Laurel groaned and mentally crossed off the stew. There was a grayish piece of fish floating alongside it on the plate. From the smell, it had been around camp long enough to qualify as an old friend. Laurel crossed that off, too.

She nodded casually to Estéban and strolled away, trying to look like a tourist who wanted to see the rest of the village. Fortunately, no one evinced the slightest interest in accompanying her. When she returned a little later, she was able to hand over a clean plate and calmly refuse a second helping. She *did* take a small plump banana from a clump near the stove and found it to be the best she'd ever tasted. She was still eating it when Estéban came up to her, wiping his mouth with the back of his hand.

He belched with gusto and beamed. *"Favor, senorita,"* he said, pointing to the building with the screen porch, indicating she should walk ahead of him. When she hesitated, he gestured toward the others who had now finished lunch and were off to find a convenient patch of shade. Afternoon siesta had arrived and she was to have her rest in screened comfort.

Laurel followed him to the porch steps and tried not to show her reluctance. The excitement of the trip had made her as wide awake as a freshman during finals week. When Estéban marched firmly over to the door and ushered her into a tiny cubicle, she followed with dragging steps. Certainly she couldn't sleep, but for appearances' sake she would follow the custom and not prove an embarrassing guest. She intended to tell Casey that this part of the excursion wouldn't get an enthusiastic acceptance.

She was even more convinced when Estéban gave her a brief nod of farewell and withdrew, closing the door behind him.

One glance around the room sent her spirits down to snake level. The only light in the cubicle came from a patch of screen over the solid wooden door. A candle stuck on a wooden chest of drawers provided light for any unwary visitor trapped into an overnight stay.

Laurel's gaze moved to the iron cot shoved against the far wall. She decided the thin mattress atop it whose cover was already coming apart in the humidity rated in the same league as the candle. Obviously the tour operators didn't plan for any repeat business. She pulled a wooden chair into the middle of the room to avoid some small bugs which were taking their constitutional on the wall. After brushing off the chair, she sat down, feeling like the next patient in a dentist's waiting room. She raised her wrist and managed to read the face of her watch without lighting the candle—then let her hand fall back in her lap again. Idly her glance dropped to the floor and widened as she discovered a new variety of insect meandering through the gaps in the floorboards. Laurel pulled her feet up on the rungs of the chair and deliberately closed her eyes. She'd stay put for a token twenty minutes and then return to the outdoor compound—whether the Indians were ready or not.

She still had three minutes to go and looked as stiff and lifeless as a mummy in an Egyptian tomb when the door of the hut swung open.

Casey shook his head unbelievingly as he stood on the threshold. "What's the matter—are you some kind of a nut?" he rapped out. "This is a hell of a place to go into a trance."

"Who's in a trance? Any fool could see that I was taking a siesta," she stormed back at him, blinking in the light. "They expected me to."

He stared at her. "Sitting bolt upright on a chair in the middle of a cell."

"If you'd spare another glance," she had herself under control enough to match his sarcasm, "you'll note that the bugs were already in control of the mattress . . . and the wall . . . *and* the floorboards." She moved her shoe hastily as she tacked on the last words. "Besides, you're not even supposed to be here. You're supposed to be in Calli . . . you said so."

"For God's sake, I know where I'm supposed to be. There've been some problems. I'll tell you about it on the way back." He held his watch up to the light and winced. "C'mon—we're cutting things too damned fine as it is."

She stumbled over the threshold and felt her arm taken in a painful grip as he almost yanked her down the steps. "Will you wait a minute," she appealed, trying to keep up with his long, loping strides as he cut around the building and headed straight for the path. "I have to thank these people . . . they were really very nice. And Estéban . . ."

"I've already talked to Estéban. He's on his way back to town with a message I gave him for the tour group."

"Then what's the rush?"

"The rush is," he spaced out the words so that she couldn't possibly misunderstand, "that the *Traveler* is sailing from Buenaventura on the tide. Approximately one hour from now."

Chapter Eight

The rest of that journey down the path was done without pausing and without stopping to smell any flowers along the way. Once, when Laurel had to slow down because of a stitch in her side, she said breathlessly, "I suppose I should thank you . . ."

Casey kept his arm under her elbow and shot her a suspicious glance. "Let's get to the river first. You can take care of the amenities later." He lengthened his stride. "If you've enough breath to talk, you can go faster. The captain can't change the sailing time."

That thought was so appalling that Laurel forgot about the pain in her side and managed to keep up with the chief purser's tall figure as they ran toward the row of palms which she knew bordered the river. Casey was wearing a pair of lightweight slacks and a white shirt which he'd unbuttoned halfway down his chest because of the heat. The outfit wasn't the kind any man would choose for a trek into the Colombian jungle. He must have set off on this rescue mission without taking time to change.

It wasn't until they finally reached the pier and had scrambled aboard a trim launch tied there that Laurel was able to relax. She collapsed in a cane chair under a brightly colored awning which covered the stern of the launch, as Casey moved up to talk to the man at the helm who was gunning the throttle. Another crew member in immaculate shorts and a shirt coiled the bow line by the rail. Seconds later, the helmsman had spun the wheel and was heading back down the river at full speed.

Casey finally came out on the stern and dragged another cane chair alongside Laurel's, subsiding in it with a weary sigh. For several minutes they both sat there—content to get their breath back and enjoy the breeze on their faces as the launch skimmed along. Then Casey pulled his damp shirt away from his chest and grimaced. "Too bad we don't have a clothesline aboard. We could hang ourselves up to dry."

Laurel was taking off her jacket as he spoke—too hot to care about her sodden halter top. "I know. If this water weren't so muddy, I wouldn't mind being towed on a rope behind the boat."

"At least you can hop in the pool when you get aboard the *Traveler.*" Casey's glance swept over her and then he turned his attention to rummaging for a package of cigarettes in the cotton sports jacket he'd left on the launch. "I'll have to wait for a shower tonight."

"You mean you're not getting on the ship?"

"Lord, no." He looked surprised that she'd ever thought of such an idea. "It was just a fluke that I came back this afternoon. I found Peg in a state of hysterics because they'd moved the sailing time forward. She knew that you'd return to an empty pier so she was trying to round up the company man at Buenaventura to take care of you."

"Except that the company man was with you . . . supposedly on the way to Calli." Laurie's eyes darkened at the idea of being stranded. "I didn't even bring my passport with me and my traveler's checks are all aboard . . ."

"It's all right, love." Casey's voice was matter-of-fact as he lit a cigarette and flipped the match over the side. "We didn't throw you away, so don't have nightmares about it."

She knew that he was being brusque deliberately, so she tried to keep her voice just as casual. "The only thing I'll have nightmares about is sitting in that horrible room with all those bugs," she said. "Incidentally, if you want to keep Marden passengers happy, I'd skip the jungle tour. Either that or furnish trail bikes and box lunches. I'm all for organic food—but frankly I think monkey stew is overdoing it."

"Good God!" Casey shook his head despairingly. "I'm sorry, Laurel—I didn't realize or I'd never have asked you to go."

"Lunch wasn't *that* bad." She felt she could show a little warmth after his handsome apology. "I must say you do better in the boat line than I do." Her gesture took in the modern launch and its immaculate condition.

"That's another thing," Casey said soberly. "I had no idea that they'd switch boats on you. Peg shouldn't have allowed you to go in that thing."

"Don't make me sound like a complete incompetent. Besides, Estéban was very nice."

"So's a dugout canoe but not for a jaunt like this." He drew on his cigarette and concluded morosely. "What a day this has been! Lousy—all the way."

She managed a crooked smile. "There was a medicine man back with the friendly Indians. You should have asked for time on his couch. He could have fitted in an appointment between the native dances."

"Keep that up and you'll get that river bath you mentioned."

Her smile deepened as she pushed her hair back to let the breeze cool her throat. "I still want to know why you came back to the ship at the crucial moment."

"Because a band of Indians on the road to Calli weren't feeling as friendly as your chums. Seems some young braves were unhappy about the price they're being paid for their fishing catch so they'd barricaded a main bridge. This morning they were shooting at any cars attempting to get through." He grinned at her shocked expression. "We didn't argue when the *policia* turned us back."

"What will you do now?"

"The last I heard, we'll fly up in a private plane when I return." He stood up and prowled the deck restlessly. "I'm a hell of a lot more concerned about you."

He sounded so unlike himself that Laurel shot him a puzzled look from under her lashes. Either the heat was getting to him or he was thoroughly annoyed at being dragged into the rescue mission.

Impulsively she stood up and went over to join him by the rail of the launch. "I didn't mean to act like such a jellyfish," she said hesitantly. "Instead of complaining about the lunch menu, I should have been thanking you for the rescue."

After she'd finished, she braced herself for the

typical Casey Waring response—first the derisive glance and then the usual banter of how she could repay him on the return voyage. Strangely enough, it didn't come.

Instead he kept his glance on an island they were passing in the middle of the river as he said, "Forget it. It was no big deal. I couldn't very well go off and leave you stranded." He turned then and grinned at her. "Believe it or not, my mother was a great reader of Emily Post. She had me looking for little old ladies to help across the street until I was twenty." His mouth twisted in a wry smile. "After that, I looked for younger ones."

Laurie met his gaze frankly. "All I know is that I'm glad you came down my street today." As he stared down at her, she continued shyly. "I wasn't going to admit it—but those deserted islands in the river *are* intriguing. It must be all this solitude . . ." She gestured around them. "When you combine it with the palm trees and sunshine, it's a pretty heady combination. I know all the drawbacks are still there," she went on with a rush, "but I'm really sorry we didn't have time for our outing."

Casey's jaw went tight—then he swung back to sit in his cane chair and say lightly, "It's just as well. We'd probably both end up with sunstroke . . . along with the mosquito bites." He must have seen her chagrin because he burst out, "Damn it all—I didn't mean it. Nothing about this trip is turning out the way I planned. And after finding you in that stinking camp, I don't know whether I'm on my head or my heels." He gave a snort of disgust. "The worst part is—I couldn't care less." He leaned toward her and put his hands on his knees. "Believe me, love—the way things stand between us—being on one of those islands with you would be really looking for trouble."

Laurel's glance fell in confusion before his. She knew her heart was pounding and her palms were clammy . . . despite the temperature.

Casey must have sensed her despair because he stubbed out his cigarette and went on quietly. "Now it's time to hear from the home team. Was I right? Be honest, Laurel. How do you feel about us?"

She bit down hard on her lower lip and her voice was tremulous as she admitted. "Awful. Right now, my stomach feels as if I'd eaten that monkey stew." At his involuntary shout of laughter, she smiled reluctantly. "You're the only man who's ever made me lose my appetite! And don't tell me I should be thankful."

"Wouldn't think of it. I feel a little bruised and battered myself." He got up as he spoke and came over by the rail to put an arm around her shoulders. Laurel stiffened instinctively, but when he simply rested his chin against her hair, she let her body relax.

"We'll have to do something about it, love." His voice was muffled as he kept her close against him, "But this isn't the place. Nothing like going for a boat ride on our day off." He felt her weak chuckle and pushed her back to arm's length. "Talk about a pair of idiots!"

"I know. As long as confessions are in order—I'm glad to discover I have company in my misery. At least you had Gwen to console you in the past."

"And you had Eduardo. Every time I looked, he wasn't more than six inches away. With honorable intentions, too." He glanced at her severely. "The worst kind."

She couldn't help laughing. "I didn't have to worry about that with Gwen."

He was prompt in confirming it. "You're right. She's the safest kind of woman . . . understands all the rules."

"Meaning I don't?"

"There's no comparison. You know it." He flicked the end of her nose with his finger and put her safely away from him. "That's all I'm saying for now . . . so you can damn well stop fishing."

"I don't see how you've survived this long," she said, exasperated. "Some woman should have put strychnine in your coffee years ago."

"You can always try. Let's not fight, Laurie," he went on coaxingly. "It's too nice being with you without a hundred people staring at us over their shoulders."

"Or complaining about their stateroom furniture." When he cocked a warning eyebrow, she held up her hand. "Don't say it . . . I'll be good. Take no notice of my lapses."

"I could do with a few more of them." He reached out to pull her down into the chair beside him. "If it weren't for the temperature and that boatman keeping his eagle eye on us, we could do better than this. Unfortunately, South Americans frown on public demonstrations of affection and he'd be shocked to the marrow if I pulled you on my lap." He captured her fingers in a firm grip, "But I'm damned if I'll ignore *all* the side benefits in this newfound state of affairs."

Laurel kept her eyes down, unwilling to confess even now how his nearness affected her. When he'd held her by the rail, she'd wanted to burrow her head against his chest in sudden despair because she knew then how much she loved him. Desired him achingly—whatever his terms—and it was all she could do to keep from shouting it to the skies. Now she had to sit quietly and hope she hadn't read too much into his few words.

She felt his fingers moving gently under her chin. "Aren't you ever going to look at me again, honey?" he chided.

One encounter with his quizzical masculine gaze was enough to make her glance quickly away in confusion. Perhaps all her crazy hopes were justified, after all. The look on Casey's face showed plainly that he would prefer to be doing other things. It didn't take much imagination to guess what they might be.

After that, the ride back down the river passed in silence, but with a newfound awareness and contentment between them. When the scattered buildings of Buenaventura appeared at the large inlet, Laurel came back to reality at the sight of the empty pier ahead of them.

"Casey, the ship's gone," she moaned. "The *Traveler*'s sailed. What do I do now?"

"It's all right, my love. See that launch coming toward us from midstream? He's been expecting us. Everything's okay now." He gave her fingers a reassuring squeeze.

"I still don't understand . . ."

"That's the pilot launch. The *Traveler* will be going dead slow outside the breakwater and they'll put you aboard when the pilot comes off. Captain Samuels knows all about it, so you don't have to worry. The immigration officials do it all the time. My only worry was whether we'd get back in time to make the connection." He glanced at his watch. "We shaved it pretty close. I'll have to buy them a beer the next time I'm down this way."

"What will *you* do? Will you catch your flight?"

"Don't worry about me." He grinned down at her. "See that character in the white suit on the pier making threatening gestures."

She nodded.

"Well," Casey drawled, "I'll buy him two beers after keeping him cooling his heels this long." As the man at the wheel of their launch cut his speed to go alongside the trim cutter with *"Pilota"* written on the wheelhouse, Casey added reluctantly, "We'd better go amidships. I'll help you across."

Laurel stood up and felt his arm at her waist immediately to steady her as the launch hit the pilot boat's wake.

"Be careful! I don't want to lose you now," Casey teased. "Not after all the time I've invested in you."

She copied his tone. "And energy. From the sound of things, I'll owe you at least two beers."

"I'll take you up on it. How about paying off in Lima?"

"On our official nightclub tour?" she asked solemnly.

"No way, honey." He was braced against the rail but he took time to say cheerfully, "I can still manage my courting without a tour guide, thanks. Is it a date, then?" His last words came out quietly.

Laurel couldn't speak over the sudden lump in her throat but she nodded as she met his glance.

He gripped her fingers hard in response and then turned to acknowledge the shout of the man at the wheel of the pilot launch.

"Casey! *Por amor de Dios—pronto, hombre!*" He signaled the purser to help Laurel across to the waiting crewman on his boat.

"Okay, Paco—keep your shirt on," Waring called back.

"Tres cervezas, Casey!" The other raised three fingers as he grinned broadly.

Casey took time out for a derisive gesture. Then his face sobered quickly as he grasped Laurel around the waist. "Take care of yourself, my love," he told her gruffly and swung her across to the other launch as the two hulls momentarily came together.

Laurel felt another strong pair of arms grasp her waist in the instant before the two boats drew apart.

Casey signaled the "all clear" to the helmsman, *"Mil gracias, Paco."*

"De nada, Casey. *Buena suerte."*

Waring brought his hand up in a salute but his somber gaze was on Laurel as he called a final *"Hasta la vista"* before the broadening waters of the Agua Dulce made any further contact impossible.

It was that last sight of Casey's desolate figure aboard the launch that occupied Laurel's thoughts and reflected her feelings on the trip out to the *Traveler*. When the big familiar hull finally loomed ahead of the pilot boat, the muddy cast of the Agua Dulce had changed to the gray-green of the mighty Pacific and the humid inland air had been supplanted by a biting salt breeze which had the official flag on the *Traveler*'s main mast stretched at full length.

As the pilot boat circled the stern to come alongside, Laurel heard shouts of welcome and looked up to see a gallery of heads and waving arms. Until then, she'd forgotten that seeing the pilot off was one of the pleasures cruise passengers alloted for themselves. Now that they had identified Laurel's figure, this transfer had extra spice. While not consciously hoping that either the pilot or Laurel would get dunked in the changing process, they all hung over the rail making sure that they didn't miss a thing, just in case it happened.

Fortunately the exchanges were made in a swift, efficient fashion. The only water clinging to Laurel as she climbed aboard the *Traveler* was the salt mist in her hair. She heard a cheer from the upper decks as the Colombian pilot also dropped safely to the deck of the launch. A few minutes later she waved as Paco grinned up at her before circling away from the ship.

Peg, Eduardo, and Elena were waiting for her at the stair landing on the pool deck.

"Thank heavens!" Peg cried dramatically. "If you hadn't made it aboard, I think Casey would have cut me up for fish bait the next time he saw me."

"If he hadn't, then I would," Eduardo put in, sounding terse. He stared down at Laurel's tired face and shook his head. "You look as if you've been exploring the Amazon for two weeks rather than the Agua Dulce for a day. I don't know what Casey was thinking about!"

Laurel defended herself. "I'll be perfectly fine

after I have a shower and some food. Actually everyone was wonderful to me. If it hadn't been so hot . . ."

"I'll take you to your stateroom," Elena told her, exhibiting the most sense of any of them. "There's plenty of time for talking later on."

"She's right . . . we have two days until Lima," Eduardo said.

"Plenty of time to get you back in fighting shape," Peg agreed. "Extra vitamins with your meals and early to bed."

"Don't make me sound like a stretcher case," Laurel protested. "You've been seeing too many of those old movies Casey brought aboard where the heroine dies of consumption in the last reel." She put up a finger to test the skin on her nose. "At least I'm going to have the best sunburn on the ship."

"And plenty of time in the shade to get over it," Peg said as they paused in the foyer. "Casey told me he wants an inventory of the stock room by the time we get to Lima. He suggested that I recruit you and Elena . . ."

"What's this 'recruit'?" the younger girl asked suspiciously.

"Another word for volunteer," Eduardo said, chuckling. "I'm leaving before Peg decides to 'recruit' me, too."

"I might have known," the doctor's wife sighed. "You sound like George."

"Just showing good masculine sense. However, I'll make amends by buying you all a drink in a half hour. Does that sound good to you, *Laurita mia*?"

Her deep blue eyes smiled back at him. Now

that she was on familiar ground with friends around—plus the memory of her launch trip with Casey to sustain her—she decided that life was good. Very good, indeed. "It sounds wonderful," she said emphatically. "Thanks, Eduardo. I wouldn't miss it for anything."

The next days at sea on the way to Lima were marvelous therapy. Only the weather deteriorated as the ship moved past the equator and hit a series of swells off the coast. Patches of thick fog left the deck chairs dripping until the afternoon winds came up, sending the mist on its way and drying the open decks. A pale sun finally won out so the swimming pool brigade could get in their toasting time.

That was the day Peg shepherded Elena and Laurel down to the chief purser's storeroom close by the surgery and handed them typewritten lists. "Now we count. Elena—you start with the bridge tallies and cards . . . all the game supplies. Laurel, do you have any 'druthers'?"

The other shook her head. "Makes no difference to me." She was admiring a crepe-paper bird costume hanging with some others on a hook at the side of the room. "I didn't see these at the party the other night."

"They're just extras," Peg said. "Casey keeps them for the people who don't like to make things but still want to take part in the costume parties. All cruise ships do. Of course, it isn't strictly fair to the others, but the results are better. Facilities for designing costumes aboard ship are pretty limited." She turned to Laurel. "You know what I mean after judging the other night."

"Well, there were an awful lot of sequins on net skirts . . ."

"Exactly. That reminds me"—Peg glanced at her watch and moved toward the door—"I'll be up in the lounge if you hit a problem."

"You mean—you aren't 'recruited' for this, too?" Elena complained, looking up from a box full of bridge score pads.

"Sorry, sweetie." To her credit, Peg did sound remorseful. "My craft class—remember. The ladies are still gluing 'jewels' on everything in sight. I'll be down as soon as the class is over." She glanced around the storeroom and sighed. "It looks to me as if we'll spend the rest of the trip down here. I didn't realize the inventory was going to be such a job."

"It doesn't matter to me," Laurel confessed. "After loafing so long, it's rather nice to have something to do."

Peg stared at her as if she were some kind of strange species. "That's a funny attitude for somebody who's on a vacation, I must say."

Laurel smiled but didn't argue. She couldn't very well admit that she welcomed being kept busy so that she wouldn't have time to count each passing minute until she met Casey again. Even now, the memory of their trip down the Agua Dulce made her heart leap around like a college cheer leaders. The thoughts of the greater pleasures in store were so exciting that she had trouble behaving naturally.

And that was one thing she was determined to do under the circumstances. Their newly acknowledged relationship was still far too delicate to be subjected to gossip and shipboard speculation.

The truth was Laurel herself didn't know what would happen in the future. She had a suspicion that some of her beliefs would topple like the walls of Jericho on the return voyage, but for the moment, she had to trust in Casey's judgment and decency. She smiled ruefully. Since she seemed to fall under a spell as soon as she came close to him, it was the only thing to do.

It was approaching dusk on the second afternoon when the lights and buildings of Callao—the port city for the Peruvian capital of Lima—showed on the coastline. As the *Traveler* moved into the shore waters and slowed to pick up the pilot, the outlines of a small fleet of warships could be seen at anchor ahead of them.

"The Peruvian navy," she heard one of the passengers who'd lived in South America remark. "It's always on display in the same place. I don't think they can move it. There's a rumor among the natives that all the ships have glass bottoms."

"At least they save on the defense budget that way," someone else said. "They're ready for a quick civilian conversion, too. All they have to do is schedule visitor tours on Sundays."

The first man grinned his appreciation. "They wouldn't get many customers—there are too many other interesting things to do around here. Lima's a fabulous city—don't miss their Museum of Gold if you're touring tomorrow."

"I won't." His friend was peering over the rail watching the pilot boat disgorge officials. "Those two fellows coming aboard with the briefcases must be the Peruvian bankers we heard about."

"That's right. They'll change your money from dollars to *soles*—the official currency here. And for God's sake—don't try to use anything else while you're in the country. I remember one fellow who decided to beat the black market and got himself thrown in the pokey."

Laurel moved determinedly away before the end of the story. What she wanted just then was a chance to enjoy coming into Callao in peace and quiet. She took the elevator to the upper deck and dodged the cluster of excited passengers in the Inca Lounge who were trying to decide whether to go into Lima after dark or wait until the next morning for their tour. As she climbed the outside stairway to the flying bridge, she saw that it was deserted as usual—probably because of the stiff wind that buffeted her when she reached the top steps. Because of its force, she paused to put a scarf over her head before she approached the rail. While she was still tying the silk square, she caught the mumble of masculine voices from the bridge deck below. She smiled as she found herself an unwilling eavesdropper once again and had just decided to move to the other side of the ship when the word "Casey" kept her where she was.

"You mean Casey didn't come aboard with the pilot?" It was easy to identify Captain Samuels' querulous tones. "Why in the hell is he changing plans now?"

"He isn't." It was the chief officer who replied. "This radiogram just confirms that he'll come aboard tomorrow morning. At least we know that he's in Lima. For a while there, I had doubts he'd get out of Colombia in time."

"Well, if he's here, why isn't he coming aboard when we anchor? There's a Marden freighter docked alongside our pier." The captain sounded irate. "I don't want to stick around entertaining their passengers tonight—that's Casey's bag."

"Give the second purser the duty."

"He's not as good as Casey."

"Yeah, but Casey's having his own party tonight. Remember María Origa—that gorgeous brunette from Santiago who was aboard on the last cruise?"

"The one whose father was in shipping?" The captain's tone warmed. "You bet! She arranged the party at the embassy that night. You mean she's waiting around here for Casey?"

"All I know is that she's in Lima now and I can't see Casey deserting her for a duty dinner aboard ship." Jensen's voice wasn't as clear when they evidently started to move back into the closed bridge. "I got the idea that Senor Origa was anxious to add our chief purser to the family. Maybe María can convince Casey to stay down here on this trip."

"She could convince me without half trying," the captain said. "But since nobody's sending any job offers or brunettes our way, we'd better get back to work. I want to see that new duty roster before you post it . . ." His voice faded to an indistinct mumble and then ceased completely.

Laurel stood quietly in the silence that followed and then walked over to the rail to stare blindly down at the water surging past the hull as the *Traveler* regained speed with the pilot aboard.

She was grateful for the solitude that surrounded her on the bridge although the conversation had left no visible outward effect. Only a close onlooker would have noticed the rigid way she held her lips to keep them from trembling and the desperate control on her features. There was no way to rationalize her hurt pride or the desolation that washed over her. Like a seventh wave creating havoc in its wake—the news that Casey had still another woman on his string left Laurel too miserable to struggle with her emotions any longer.

The only alternative was to acknowledge her defeat and retreat as quickly and painlessly as possible.

Once Laurel had decided, it was amazing how efficiently she functioned. She waited in line in the main lounge to change her dollars into Peruvian money and managed to carry on a lighthearted conversation with Elena and Eduardo at the same time. When the financial transaction was finished, the *Traveler* was already berthed at its Callao pier. Avoiding the main gangway which was thronged with debarking passengers and Peruvian officials, she made her way forward to the crew gangway on a lower deck. There she found a young Peruvian guard standing by a telephone which had just been connected.

"I hope you speak English," she said, going over beside the young man. "It'll make this a lot easier."

"I took it in school," he replied proudly. "Is there something I can do for you, senorita? Maybe you'd like to learn about our tourist attractions . . ."

"No, thanks," she remarked. "I understand there's a daily flight from Lima to the States. Could you call and get me a reservation on that plane tonight?"

He winced as if in pain. "Plane reservations are very difficult in Peru. Many people wait for weeks to get space."

"I realize that," she said in an implacable tone that her friends wouldn't have recognized. "Therefore, I'm prepared to pay." She drew out a bundle of Peruvian currency and put it down next to the telephone. "Spend what you need and keep whatever is left. You might have to offer a premium to secure a cancellation."

His eyes surveyed her somberly. "This flight is important to you, senorita?"

"Very important." She made no move to explain further and he didn't seem to expect it.

He pulled a notebook from his pocket. "Then I'll do my best. Where can I reach you?"

Laurel gave him the number of her stateroom and, satisfied she'd done all that was possible, went up to eat a dinner she didn't want. Afterwards, she pleaded fatigue to Eduardo and the Purcells and went down to finish packing her belongings. She had just closed the suitcase she planned to take with her and tagged her other luggage for dead storage when a knock came on the stateroom door.

The young guard was waiting outside in the corridor. "You were fortunate, senorita. I have a place for you on the midnight flight. A man I know who works at the airport was able to secure a cancellation." He smiled slightly. "Our soccer team is booked on the plane and one of the players decided to postpone his flight for a day. You can pick up your ticket at the airport, but I'd suggest your leaving now. Otherwise, things happen..."

"I'm ready. Where can I get a taxi?"

"There'll be one at the end of the pier, senorita. I'm going off duty now so I can carry your luggage if it's ready."

"Thank you. There's just one piece. I'll get it for you." She turned and went back into the stateroom, returning almost immediately with the bag in her hand. "Give me five minutes and I'll meet you at the end of the pier. There's a phone call I must make."

"Bueno," he nodded politely and took the bag.

Laurel's phone call was to the chief officer and luckily she found him in his quarters. After identifying herself, she explained that a sudden emergency necessitated her leaving for home on the first flight out. When he would have questioned her further, she said hurriedly that she hoped to see him at the steamship offices the next time the *Traveler* was in port. In the meantime, if he'd offer her apologies to all concerned, she'd be most grateful. The chief officer replied in some surprise that he certainly would and heard a soft click in his ear before he could say anything more.

Laurel then checked her purse to make sure that she had her passport and traveler's checks, put on her coat, and let herself out the stateroom door.

As she went down the *Traveler*'s gangway for the final time, she felt as if she were walking away from her entire world—away from its shelter and protection—into a frightening unknown. But if all the familiar faces and comforts disappeared at the bottom of the gangway, then surely some of the despair and misery stopped there, too.

Laurel kept her eyes lowered to the rough cement as she walked along a pier lit by spotlights fastened on the towering loading cranes. Any final glances up toward the promenade deck and the flying bridge would be simple indulgence on her part. She couldn't close her ears though, to the music of "Tie a Yellow Ribbon Round the Old Oak Tree," which suddenly floated down from the record player in the lounge. The melody with all its nostalgic associations was a blow she hadn't expected.

Then she saw the guard with the taxi waiting by the pier gates and she almost ran the rest of the distance.

Eventually the time would come when she'd feel human again, she told herself. After she'd run far enough—flown far enough, and finally immersed herself in the mind-dulling routine at home.

Only after that would she dare to reexamine her mangled emotions. Maybe even salvage some pieces from the broken bits. Then she'd acknowledge how much falling in love could hurt and put up warnings never to be smug and complacent about it again. She'd find new friends and start all the exciting projects she'd never gotten around to.

There was only one other thing she could do to complete the cure—make sure that she never came into contact with a man like Casey Waring again. That was the most important rule of all.

Chapter Nine

Laurel returned to work in San Francisco two days later.

She pleaded a family emergency as the reason for her hasty departure from Lima. Since her employers were considerate and realistic individuals, they didn't query the obvious loopholes in her excuse. Instead they listened with interest to her suggestions for improving passenger activities on future cruises and suggested she incorporate some of them in the new brochure which was in the works. The excursion to the Friendly Indians on the Agua Dulce was regretfully but firmly canceled.

Laurel was mildly surprised that no one asked about internal affairs on the *Traveler* since she had been requested to watch for anything unusual before she left on the cruise. Ten days passed and the *Traveler* was due back in Long Beach the next day before the manager of the passenger division finally called her into his office to discuss the subject. When he asked if she'd discovered anything that might prove valuable on the smuggling situation, Laurel could only say that the officers of the *Traveler* tried everything in their power to discourage contraband activities.

"Discourage it—sure," her chief said. "But that's a far cry from stopping it. Smuggling costs the company money, it costs the government money, and everybody's unhappy. What we need is a good old-fashioned miracle to solve our problems."

Laurel thought of mentioning the two incidents that had occurred on the trip and then changed her mind. The affair on the dock at Manzanillo was Casey Waring's business and there wasn't an ounce of proof that her experience in El Salvador had sinister overtones. Like so many things on that cruise, it was best forgotten.

The man on the other side of the desk saw her hesitation and guessed the reason for it. His reports from the *Traveler* on the outward voyage were far more exhaustive than she realized. "You heard that Dr. Purcell is being relieved of his duties after this trip?" he asked casually.

"Yes . . . someone told me."

"I doubt if they mentioned that he was involved in a smuggling incident some months ago on the ship. A kilo of cocaine was found among the medical supplies, but there was no proof the doctor knew anything about it."

"Then his dismissal isn't linked to that?"

He shook his head. "Dr. Purcell drinks too much," he said flatly. "Any doctor has to be dependable, but it's absolutely vital for a ship's doctor. Fortunately, George realizes it."

"Is he leaving the ship at Long Beach this trip?"

"No—he and his wife will change over here in San Francisco. We have a replacement ready. Waring settled that before he left."

Laurel felt a stirring of panic at the announcement but battened down on it firmly. Her voice was controlled as she said, "Left? I don't understand. What happened to the chief purser? Did he get off the ship at Lima, after all?"

"Casey! In Lima? Hell, no! He left the *Traveler* in El Salvador this week. Our New York office wanted to hear his report in person." He surveyed her carefully. "What's all this about his staying in South America?"

She gestured apologetically, "Just ship's gossip . . . some rumor was going round."

"You should have known better than to pay attention to that." He pulled a manila folder toward him on the desktop and opened it. "Anyhow, Casey's departure has left a hole in the ship's personnel. That's why I want you to go down and meet the *Traveler* in Long Beach. Give them a hand with the paperwork on the trip up here. It's just a day and a night so it won't put you behind in your department here." He looked up in time to see her stricken expression. "What's the matter? Any reason why you can't go?"

Laurel put her features in order. "No. I suppose I can collect the luggage I left aboard at the same time. I'd planned on sending for it when the *Traveler* docked here."

"Well, then this is a good thing all around. If you fly to Los Angeles in the morning, there should be ample time. The ship has to clear Customs and discharge cargo and passengers when they dock. They won't sail until later in the day." He stood up to signify the discussion was finished. "Captain Samuels is expecting you. Have a good trip. I'll see you when you get back."

Despite her outward submission, Laurel was still feeling rebellious the next afternoon as her taxicab neared the city pier in Long Beach harbor where the Marden ships berthed.

Since she had, with every good intention in the world, vowed never to go near the *Traveler* again, it was frustrating to find herself staring at the gray funnel now. Of course she had to be realistic; the main reason for those vows wasn't on the ship—he was a safe six thousand miles away, which made her reluctance both illogical and immature. And Laurel had a very good idea how her boss would have reacted if she'd declined to come.

By the time the taxi turned into the gate of the pier to pull alongside the warehouse and Customs area, she was able to view the *Traveler*'s big hull with resignation if not outright enthusiasm.

When she paid off the cab and made her way hesitantly into the section of the building marked VISITORS, the first person she met was Ted Jensen.

"By God, Laurel Cavanaugh!" The chief officer's broad face beamed as he got up off an empty table designated for Customs men and came over to shake hands enthusiastically. "The captain said you'd be coming along. Glad to see you again."

"It's good to see you, Ted." To her surprise, Laurel found that she meant every word. "How was the trip from Lima?"

"A little on the dull side. There's never as much excitement as outward bound for the passengers." He ran a finger around the collar of his khaki uniform shirt and impatiently surveyed the empty scene around them. "After waiting an hour and a half for the *Traveler* to clear here before they can even start going through Customs, we'll never get them on a ship again."

"I wondered why everything was so deserted." She stared past the tables to an enclosure where a few relatives and friends were waiting on benches. The only Customs men visible lounged by their makeshift office while waiting for the passenger debarkation. "What's holding things up?"

"Another Customs search." The chief officer sat down heavily on the end of a table and motioned for her to join him. "Somebody got the word that we're carrying a big shipment of hot cargo. As a result the Canine Corps and the two-legged sleuths have gone over the crew and cargo decks inch by inch. Every dirty laundry bag has been pulled apart—every crewman's stateroom searched. They've even invaded the frozen food lockers and checked the supplies." He sighed, looking like a man who was thoroughly sick of the subject. "I had to handle liaison—that's why I'm here rather than aboard."

"You're good at things like that," she said, trying to bolster his spirits.

"Well, I've had plenty of practice on this trip. You let me in for a good share when I announced that you'd turned tail in Lima. Eduardo threatened to sue the company until I gave him your address in San Francisco and that gal ... Elena something or other ..."

"Elena Sanchez."

"That's the one. She was crushed because her parents didn't have a chance to meet you. Apparently they're coming to call on you in San Francisco, too. Casey smoothed that over."

Laurel's knuckles turned white as she gripped the strap of her purse. "Was he upset?"

Jensen's thick eyebrows climbed. "Casey? Not

that I remember. You just missed him by a couple hours. I suppose you heard that he flew back to the East Coast?" At her nod, he went on, "We'll learn in San Francisco, if he's staying back there–" He broke off as a group of Customs men suddenly appeared at the top of the gangway. "Looks as if they're finally set to release the passengers. Another dry run, I'd guess."

Laurel stood up beside him while they watched the Customs men come down the gangway. "Ted . . ." she caught at his arm as he started to move forward. "What will they be looking for now? On the dock, I mean?"

He frowned. "The usual things passengers try to get away with . . . undeclared art objects passed off as souvenirs . . . emerald rings buried in cold cream . . . small-time stuff. Not the big haul everybody expected."

"They'll find plenty of jewels," Laurel commented. "The ladies were sewing them on for two solid weeks in Peg's classes. Remember that costume ball? Half the outfits were covered with them."

He started to laugh. "I'd rather forget it. You might as well go back to Long Beach and enjoy life for a few more hours. We won't sail until seven and then we only move to Terminal Island for refueling. If you get back aboard by–" he broke off as he saw her intent expression. "What's the matter, girl? Did you forget something?"

"No . . . just the opposite." Laurel's forehead creased as she tried to think. "Tell me, Ted–what happens to the passengers who stay aboard? Does their stuff go through Customs here?"

He shook his head. "No–it's examined when

they debark. That'll be tomorrow night in San Francisco or the following morning if we're delayed getting in. Why do you ask?"

She ignored his last question. "Will there be another big search there?"

"I shouldn't think so. There's no big deal when a few passengers go ashore in San Francisco." His eyes narrowed. "What's on your mind, Laurel?"

"I was just thinking that nobody would pay any attention to those costumes hanging in the purser's main storeroom—especially since they're not being taken off the ship today."

"That's right." His voice was just as terse as hers. "Keep talking."

"I'll bet if you have the Customs men look in there now, they'll find a harem costume stored with the rest. A harem costume that will eventually be taken ashore in San Francisco tomorrow. Only then it will be in a suitcase with a stack of other outfits from costume balls."

The chief officer nodded with understanding. "And a belt made up of pretty green stones wouldn't get a second look."

"Especially if the luggage belonged to the doctor's wife who served as part-time social director on the cruise." Laurel's glance was unhappy. "Ted, if I'm wrong—will you please forget that I ever said anything?"

"*If* you're wrong, then this conversation never took place. But somehow, I don't think you are." He shoved his hands in his pockets and paused for a last comment before intercepting the Customs men. "I just wish I could go into town with you for the afternoon. Frankly, I'd rather not see Doc

Purcell's face when Peg is confronted with the evidence."

It was much later that night when the *Traveler* was eased alongside a wooden platform at Terminal Island and the vibration from the engines stopped. From her vantage point by the windows in the main lounge, Laurel decided to go outside to watch the refueling operation. It was something to do and she was so desperate by then that most anything would have served.

The few passengers aboard ship for the trip north were still in shock after learning that Peg Purcell had been arrested for attempting to smuggle a fortune in cut emeralds into the United States earlier that afternoon. Dr. George Purcell was removed from the ship under sedation after learning of his wife's complicity. His departure electrified the watching passengers, and news of the affair spread through the ship with the speed of a grass fire. It was told to Laurel as she came up the gangway in the evening and was the only topic of conversation at dinner afterwards. Unfortunately, the next day's arrival of the *Traveler* in San Francisco had forced the passengers to retreat reluctantly to their staterooms. It was time to stuff their belongings into suitcases that had suddenly shrunk in the salt air.

Only Miss Scott and Laurel had remained topside in passenger territory. Miss Scott, who apparently chose to ignore packing the way she ignored her uncombed coiffure, was deep in the final chapter of a lurid novel. Laurel restlessly prowled the lounge around her, trying to overcome the loneliness that she had suffered ever since she came aboard.

From the bartender who was taking inventory of his liquor, she learned that the captain's wife had flown down from San Francisco and was now occupying a cabin on the upper deck. In the same casual tone, the bartender added that the Countess had left the ship unexpectedly that afternoon. Miss Harper had invited her to a house party in Malibu. Laurel muttered something conventional and moved off without commenting further. Apparently the Countess's interlude had played out to its hopeless conclusion.

When the ship finally berthed at Terminal Island, she opened the glass doors of the lounge and made her way steadily upward to her favorite aerie.

The panorama that stretched before her eyes when she reached the top of the ship justified the effort. The heavily populated hills surrounding the area were banded by the usual white street lights but the pink vapor lights of the freeways added a misted softness to the scene. Closer down in the harbor area itself, steam rose gently from chimneys at the industrial plants. In the darkness, their filmy gray ribbons were things of beauty rather than the pollution threats of the day.

Red warning lights outlined the superstructure of a bridge nearby, and as Laurel lowered her glance she saw a solitary gull sweep over the calm backwater where the *Traveler* was berthed. The bird's route was pinpointed by the pier searchlights which illuminated the surface during the refueling. The only sound on the bridge was the thud of a loose rope hitting the metal mast at uneven intervals. Then, distinctly, the chime of a nearby church bell floated poignantly across the harbor. The *Traveler*'s only response was the rumble of her ventilator motors.

Minutes later, the heavy equipment creaked as the ship listed when the ballast changed; the hull edged awkwardly against the dock, straining at the lines as if impatient to be gone. Laurel walked over to the port side to watch the activity below.

The refueling platform looked ludicrously like a mammoth gas station with the chief officer watching the huge rubber transfer tube just as a motorist would watch his car gas tank being filled. She felt a surge of laughter in her throat when the third mate joined him and kicked idly at the tube like a man checking the pressure on his rear tire. At any moment, she half expected to see a man shimmy up the side of the ship and start washing the windows of the dining salon.

Then she saw the chief officer turn to greet a man in a light gray suit who was carrying a topcoat in one hand and a suitcase in the other. The third mate moved over to shake hands, too, and a steward came hurrying down the gangway to take the bag.

"Casey!" The word emerged softly—unbelievingly—from Laurel's lips, but the tall man on the dock raised his head as if she'd shouted his name to the skies. When he located her figure up at the rail, he muttered abruptly to the other officers and loped up the gangway with long strides that had him out of sight in no time.

Laurel turned back to the shelter of the glass-fronted bridge without even being aware of the movement. A feeling of sheer unadulterated joy rocketed through her, and every coherent thought was swept away by the knowledge that Casey wasn't six thousand miles away—he was here and on his way to her.

As footsteps pounded up the afterdeck stairs, she flew to meet him, scattering every painful resolution and proclamation of female independence in her wake. Then his arms were around her so tightly that she almost gasped.

"Oh, Laurel . . . my dearest love . . ." He rocked her gently back and forth as he pressed his cheek against her hair. "Ten days," he murmured finally, straightening to take a deep breath. "It seemed like ten years. I should beat you for running out on me."

Laurel suddenly remembered the reason for her flight, but under the present circumstances it didn't seem to matter. "I heard that you were with a woman in Lima," she said gently, "so I didn't think you'd care."

"I cared." He pried her chin up so that she had to look at him and said with slow conviction. "What's more important—I always will. Remember that, my darling." Then he kissed her.

If she hadn't been convinced by his words, his actions would have gotten the story across. Those kisses moved from her lips to her throat and then to her eyelids in a powerful and persuasive way that showed he fully intended to make up the lost time.

Finally Laurel pushed back to catch her breath. From the way Casey's arms felt, that was as far as he was allowing her to go. She burrowed her forehead in his chest. "I can't believe it—even now."

"You should have known," he said in a rough

tone that proved he was having trouble with his breathing, too. "We could have saved ourselves a hell of a lot of misery. A man is partial to having the woman he loves within shouting distance. That's why he marries her."

Her eyes were as bright as the stars just beyond the mainmast. "You love me?"

He grinned down at her . . . the mocking grin that had been her undoing from the beginning. "How about that! Honorable intentions and all. I'm surprised myself." Then, as he saw the joy that came over her face, his grin faded and he bent to cover her lips. His first touch was soft but it soon changed. As Laurel felt the warmth of his hands through the sheer material of her blouse and trembled at his caresses, his mouth hardened to part her lips. He demanded total response and capitulation and Laurel gave it gladly—knowing his surrender was as complete as her own.

It was considerably later that they got down to explanations.

As it turned out, the woman in Lima wasn't the stumbling block Laurel had feared. "I've known María's family for years," Casey said as they sat on the bench and he put his arm around her. "There was never any mention of marriage, but it seemed more . . . honorable"—he used the word almost apologetically—"to clear the decks before I proposed to you. Then I came haring back to the ship only to have Ted tell me that you were on your way to San Francisco."

"Don't be angry. I suffered enough." She leaned against his shoulder. "This is the first time I've felt like living since that night. I couldn't believe it when I saw you come aboard. Were you surprised, too?"

"Hardly. You're the victim of a plot, my love. I called from New York to arrange it with your boss. But my flight was late and I was afraid that this time, *I'd* have to hitch a ride on the pilot's launch."

"You arranged it . . ." She couldn't get beyond his first words. "That sounds more like a vice-president than a chief purser." Her head came up. "Casey—what happened in New York?"

"Marden wants me to handle their freight operation on the West Coast. I accepted after they threw you in as a fringe benefit."

"I haven't actually heard a proposal . . ." She gave a squeak of protest as his arm tightened. "Casey!" There was a moment of silence until she was able to speak again. "Thank you very much—I'd love to."

"Ummm." He murmured with satisfaction as he buried his chin in her soft hair.

They sat in a contented silence after that until shouts from the loading platform and the rumble of a tug proved that the *Traveler* was ready to sail again. That brought the memory of the day's events back to Laurel and she sat up reluctantly. "Darling—did Ted tell you what happened today? About Peg and the doctor?"

"Yeah, I heard. The company representative gave me the story when he met me at the airport this evening. We'd thought George was the one all along." In the shadows, Casey's face was somber. "You deserve the credit for unraveling the costume dodge."

Her expression saddened. "I liked Peg . . ."

"I know." His quiet tone matched hers. "So did I. She must have gotten more desperate all the time, trying to put us off the trail. Not that we can prove anything and she certainly won't admit it. She's in enough trouble already on the smuggling charge."

"Let's forget it. There's no use doing anything else."

He nodded and pulled her to her feet. They moved over to the rail as the deck vibrated and the *Traveler* was nudged out into mid-channel.

Laurel turned to smile at the lean figure beside her. "I'm still so dazed with happiness that I can hardly believe it. Casey, darling, won't you miss going to sea?"

He heard the tremulous quiver in her voice and bent to drop a kiss on her nose. "If I do, then we'll hire a rowboat in the park. You can row."

She caught his spark of mischief. "And you can fix the dresser drawers when they stick. That takes care of our days. What about the nights?"

The vision of those glorious nights in the future with Laurel close beside him made Casey groan and reach for her again. "Believe me, dearest," he said confidently, "the way I feel about you—I can promise that the nights won't give us any trouble at all."

About the Author

Glenna Finley is a native of Washington State. She earned her degree from Stanford University in Russian Studies and in Speech and Dramatic Arts, with emphasis on radio.

After a stint in radio and publicity work in Seattle, she went to New York City to work for NBC as a producer in its international division. In addition, she worked with the "March of Time" and *Life* magazine.

As a producer, she had her own show about activities in Manhattan, a show that was broadcast to England. The programs were similar to those of the "Voice of America."

Though her life in New York was exciting, she eventually returned to the Northwest where she married. Currently residing in Seattle with her husband Donald Witte and their sons, she loves to travel, and draws heavily on her travels and experiences for the novels that have been published. Her books for NAL have sold several million copies.